The Confessions of Danny Slocum

The Confessions of Danny Slocum

A NOVEL BY
GEORGE WHITMORE

GREY FOX PRESS
SAN FRANCISCO

Cover photograph by Gregg Kitchin

Library of Congress Cataloging in Publication Data

Whitmore, George, 1945 —
   The Confessions of Danny Slocum.

   Reprint. Originally published: The Confessions of Danny
Slocum, or, Gay life in the big city. New York :
St. Martin's Press, 1980.   With new afterword.
   I. Title.
[PS3573.H527C6   1985]   813.54   85-8004
ISBN 0-912516-94-1 (pbk.)

Distributed by Subterranean Company,
P.O. Box 10233, Eugene, OR 97440

To Chuck,
with gratitude,
the many friends,
and of course,
Joe

The Confessions of Danny Slocum

I t happened again tonight. I can still smell him on the sheets. Not necessary to put my face down and sniff them. Lying in bed I can smell him. His smell is sweet, like his cum was.

When I blew him again, over by the front door, it splashed all over my face, but I washed that off when he left.

I just walked up to him and began talking. Just like that. Bought him a drink, whisked him out the door. Easy as pie. Vowed I would spend fifteen minutes, no more, in the bar, then go home alone if I struck out. I guess it worked.

Twenty or so, black-eyed, slim and trim, raven-haired. *I* came on like a combination Al Pacino/George Brent. At twenty they have no conception whatsoever of age. He was flattered, also felt he had the upper hand. I might as well have been fifty-five. (Perhaps that was part of the attraction.) In any case, I was very assertive, *very* cordial, picking him up.

Why, yes, he *was* a dancer. How did I know?

Then we were heading for my place, this dish, this very nice young man and I—chatting names, occupations, major credit cards—and it began.

That's precisely when it began, at three o'clock in the

morning, at the corner of Broadway and Seventy-fifth Street. I wondered briefly if they ran up I.D. bracelets for people like me. Like the bracelets diabetics wear in case of emergency. Because this kid should be warned. . . .

Then he lay in my arms (in all his tautness, his smoothness, his silky slinkiness, lips parted), but all I could think about was his sudden and disconcerting resemblance to— Donny Osmond, on TV. When touched in certain moanable places, he giggled disconcertingly. He had begun disconcertingly to talk baby-talk.

I knelt between his knees, cupped my hands around the flame (why write with such delicacy, Danny?) and breathed on it. It flickered, flared. (His prick was like a Roman candle, Danny, and hard in your hot hand.) He bucked and— lordy, these kids—came, and I didn't spill a drop. (It shot like gobs of hot wax against the back of your throat, Danny.)

He was kneeling over me then—how much later?— and no longer looked like Donny Osmond, was no longer talking at all, *or* giggling.

A siren, far away, spiraled up into the thick night air. The streetlight glowed Mercurochrome-orange on the shade. It had stopped raining, but the traffic on the street sounded like a torrent of rushing water. It was very quiet in the room. Then, right on cue (unlike certain happenings there in the bed) some queen staggering back from the disco began to warble:

I'm a victim of the very song I sing. . . .

My legs, resting on his thighs, began to cramp. He held my cock in his soft brown hand, tight—like the gearshift on a car.

"Aren't you going to cum?"

"I'm . . . too tired, I guess."

A challenge. He picked up the gauntlet: "I can make you." Shifted into second.

Oscillations.

My hands fluttered down to his face. "Don't. I'm getting sore."

He sat back on his heels.

"I guess I had too much to drink," I said.

He looked at me narrowly. I had been drinking club soda and he knew it.

"The fact is. . . ." I cleared my throat. "I have trouble," I whispered, ". . . cumming."

"Um," he said. Just that. The ludicrous contrast between our separate responses tonight (he was ready to go again) neither amused nor concerned him. He had simply lost interest, that fast. Which was all right with me. I didn't want to talk about it.

(This thing to which I've begun to attach such morbid significance. . . .)

And, please, if he just wouldn't start again with the hands, the mouth.

I pulled him over me and took his cock into my mouth. He pulled away, fell back, rolled off the bed. Looked like a shortstop, standing there on the balls of his feet, ready for anything.

I let my head drop onto the pillow.

He turned and picked his briefs up off the floor. Pulled them on. Jerked his head in my direction. "Still hard." An observation.

I grabbed it. "Yeah." Waved it. My hands fell back at my sides.

He was dressed. I followed him to the door. As he fumbled with the lock, I took him by the shoulders, turned him around and kissed him. He put his arms around me and hugged me tight. His kiss was (now) full of regret; mine was full of (wounded) virility.

Quickly, I knelt before him, unzipped his pants, pulled it out. It was hard. It had never really gone down.

He came again, whispering something I couldn't understand because his thighs, his jeans, were chafing my ears. He yanked it out of my mouth, just on the brink of cumming—then came, first all over the front of his T-shirt, then all over my face, then into my mouth.

He left and I locked the door. Went into the bathroom to wash off my face. Brushed my teeth. Avoided my image in the mirror.

Lying on the damp sheets, I quickly brought myself off, thinking—about something—seeing—something—not him, certainly. . . .

The sun is coming up. Raining again, softly on the tar-paper roof outside my window.

The rain in the city is *X* parts acid, I once read. The sky this morning is yellowish. I imagine the raindrops to be as well. Enough acid to erode the monuments in the park, melt them like soap. Enough acid to scald the city clean.

The roof is very black, and shiny as a piece of oilcloth. The bricks are dark, sienna-black in the dim light.

Can't sleep now. Tried to do all the things they recommend for insomnia. Finally drifted off and had a dream:

Dream of bears. I am in a state park and fending off vicious bears, hitting them on their snouts with a lady's handbag. This does not dissuade them from swiping at me with their sharp claws. Occasionally one of them will retreat into its cave, only to creep out again when I've passed by, stalk me through the forest. Where did I get the handbag?

I remember, when I moved in here, an incense smell permeated the entire apartment, evidently from perfumed candles—their drippings were all over the hearth. It drove me up the wall. I hated that smell, always so much worse when the heat actually did come on. I complained to Virgil about it. "I can't get rid of that smell." But Dr. Freud made nothing of that.

I can still smell the kid, can still taste his cum.

▲

My name is Danny Slocum.

I am a homosexual male—U.S. citizen, college-educated, thirty-three years of age, not bad-looking at all, resident of New York City. I've been around. I'm no dummy.

Yet at first I didn't realize I had a problem, a "condition." The past two years, I've cum exactly twice—in company, as it were—with two different men. I don't know how many men I've failed with in two years. . . .

But this is starting to sound like an AA speech, isn't it? A stylistic pitfall that's probably impossible to avoid. . . .

This is the record of my sex therapy.

Virgil, my shrink, suggested I keep track of my "progress" (in my state of mind everything naturally comes with quotation marks around it) in writing. He knows me well enough to know that if I don't write things down they don't seem quite real to me.

So. Sex therapy.

I'm aware that I'm another statistic, a contributor to that rising line of male impotence and dysfunction sexologists are graphing out across the face of the sexual revolution. But since I can get it up with no problem and (if I'm alone) can jack myself off without any difficulty, my "condition" wasn't apparent to me for quite a while. Wiser to ignore it. You know. These things usually go away.

But it didn't. And I didn't think Virgil himself took it that seriously. There were lots of other things to talk about. Then one day he suggested that I "work with someone."

I felt like falling to my knees and covering his hands with kisses. No shit. I was that grateful.

"A surrogate?"

"No," he said. "A partner. Someone with the same problem."

My heart was racing. I felt like crying. I hadn't realized how awful it had become.

◬

Tempted to go back through these pages (my journal, kept but sporadically for some months now) for a body count. But wouldn't I have to go back much farther, in memory, down that long line of tricks (only a few of whose faces are at all recognizable) to find the source of this dubious legacy?

Imagine that line of men, rendered in forced perspective, something like a Renaissance painting. . . . Those first distant numbers—their features are very clear to me, as clear as are his, the boy who came all over my face the other night. It's the men after those whose faces are indistinct. Did it begin with them?

I remember *him*: the first blowjob I ever gave, in college, how I gagged on it. And *him*: how he taught me how to get fucked. And *him*: I just stopped seeing him one day, but he sends me a Christmas card every year.

But then those others, those brief involvements. And then that tight knot of purely anonymous bodies, the true numbers, backed up there as if before a turnstile. Who were they? Did it begin there?

Or with the lovers?

No, I wouldn't want to count if I could, even if I had a detailed ledger. Sufficient to know for now that it was before Max, during Max, ever after Max.

▲

So it's come to this. I can't feel a thing.

"Anything wrong?"

"No. That's nice." A lie.

Think of a cool stream, slender trees just unbudding, fleecy clouds. Salem country. Marlboro country. Think of the Marlboro man. Try to relax. God, I want a cigarette. . . .

"You sure?" His face is flushed and damp.

(*Note: Sainthood to those who labor over a hard cock in vain.*)

Kiss him. Now *that's* nice.

He sits back on the bed and smiles at me. A small crease appears between his eyes. "You seem to want to. . . ."

"What?"

"Do something," he says, "you haven't told me about."

"Oh, no. Do *you* want to do something?" I ask.

He reaches for his cigarettes, puts one in his mouth, shakes one out for me. We light up.

He lies back on the bed, exhaling smoke. (*Note: Register for Smokenders; smoking is not, repeat, not sexy, contrary to the evidence before your eyes.*) His profile is to me. It's a good, clean profile. Blond forelock, smooth forehead, straight nose, full lips (a bit "too" full, the ounce of imperfection worth a pound of beauty), foursquare jaw (no nonsense), and just a sprinkling of freckles. Far more fatal to me than his struggle to make a life far away from home, than his intelligence, his newfound sophistication—the freckles.

I shake my head.

"What's wrong?"

"Nothing."

"You were shaking your head."

"Oh."

"What's wrong?"

"I don't cum."

He does not stand up and put *his* clothes on. He looks at me directly, candidly. "Well maybe next time then."

"Maybe," I say. Another lie.

&

What made me want to kiss Virgil's—my shrink's—hands in gratitude was the terror that gripped me when, with another lie, I let the blond out of my door and, unbeknown to him, out of my life. I told him, yes, I would call him because, yes, I agreed, we had so much in common and we had, yes, really enjoyed being with each other and we knew there was a chance there—for something, something very nice, I think now, too late. But I didn't call him. I knew I wouldn't. I pretended it was just another one-night stand.

What made me want to kneel before Virgil and hug his legs in gratitude was the ugly shame I felt when the blond called me and I made a date, which I broke a day later.

What made me want to cry when Virgil suggested I "work with someone" (that absurd euphemism promising further terror, too, but hope) was the stab of remorse I felt when I saw the blond on the street weeks later.

He was walking toward me, down Broadway, but as soon as he saw me he turned on his heel and walked in the opposite direction, crossed the street with nary a backward glance. Then he turned on the other side and (that remarkably decent person) gave me the finger over the roofs of the cars rushing past us, between us.

▲

So. Sex therapy.

Dinner with my novelist friend at the Riviera. He is fresh from his workout and shower at the gym across the street. Massive arms and chest pumped up to the limit under his T-shirt. And that sweet, sweet face hovering above it all.

Nice to have an excuse to come down to the Village, I say. He's just moved back down here himself after a couple of years "in exile" near me on the Upper West Side.

"You really should get yourself out of that dreary neighborhood," he says, making a face. "You'd discover sex all over again down here."

I point out that our old neighborhood is a gay ghetto itself.

(I remember *his* reason for moving down to the Village: "Every time I had a dinner party I naturally had to come down to Balducci's to shop anyway, and I realized that what I was spending on cab fare alone more than justified the higher rent. . . .")

"Speaking of sex," I say.

"Yes?" Something in my tone intrigues him. He looks up from his hamburger. The hamburger is so raw (a bodybuilder's hamburger) that blood and grease are running down his hands and dripping onto his plate.

"Sex," I say.

"Much better down here," he says. "Infinitely," tearing into the hamburger again.

I'm positive he's going to laugh at me. Danny. In sex therapy. Find something hilariously idiosyncratic and fitting about it. I remember how hard it was for me to admit to anyone that I had gone into regular therapy in the first place. Danny, the original Healthy Homosexual. That admission cost me my deep, abiding disdain for psychotherapy as the plaything of the New York middle class. But no one laughed at me then. There *was* a sly, smug undercurrent in their reactions. Yet this. . . .

"I . . . uh . . . I don't know why it's so hard for me to say this." I shove my fork into the salad I haven't eaten.

My novelist friend looks up at me over his bloody hamburger. His eyes narrow. "Wmphf?" he asks, mouth full.

"I'm going into sex therapy."

For a time his face is a complete blank. Now I'm sure he *is* going to laugh and is just clearing his mouth to do so. He swallows.

"But how *fabulous!*" he crows. (People behind him turn around and stare.) "How *fabulous!* Sex therapy!" (Hostility turns to rapt interest among the onlookers.) "How downright *American!*"

I want to pull my jacket collar over my head. Instead, I sit rigid in my chair, looking as blank as he did, as if *I* haven't been the cause of the commotion.

"Go ahead," I say. "Laugh."

He puts down his hamburger. "But darling, I'm not laughing. It's just that I can't imagine any other nationality going about it in quite the same way. Self-reliance, how-to, know-how, all that." He wipes his mouth with a paper napkin. "Of course, it *is* rather humorous. *Anything* having to do with erotic life is humorous. Don't look so chagrined. You have a problem. If you're going to change, then of course you'll have to work on it. Of course! What a marvelous adventure! I almost envy you."

Almost.

A

When this all started, I remember, I shyly began to consult my friends. I remember that, with all the charity of a registered nurse about to plunge a hypodermic needle into an upraised and defenseless buttock, my friends told me to "relax."

Ah, yes. The magic word. Never fails *them*.

▲

Am I the only one?

Here I am in the Big Apple, in an era when it seems gay life is suffering from, outrageously enough, rampant over-population. Christopher Street on a Sunday afternoon like this one presents a fleshy fantasy so sumptuous that Ingres would have blushed to paint it. Down at the Morton Street pier there is a gate in the chain-link fence between the pier proper and the street. Men are knotted in little groups on each side of the gate, waiting to get out, waiting to get in, elbowing their way through. A few intrepid straight couples, the elderly, dog-walkers brave the pier, where hundreds of semiclothed men sun, smooch, chat and watch the boats sail by on the Hudson.

Out in Bays One and Two at Riis Park, a public beach, a monument to Robert Moses, the Power Broker, who wanted a salutary haven for the recreation of New York families—out at Riis Park gay men of every color and degree are getting fried in the sun. They have brought with them styrofoam coolers, transistor radios (all the radios are playing "Love to Love You, Baby"), beach umbrellas, folding chairs and—well, the usual, but also aluminum inhalers primed with amyl nitrite and hanging around their necks from rawhide thongs. The lockers which Mr. Moses so thoughtfully provided for a nominal fee are rather out of bounds for daddies and their juniors; the locker rooms are awash nowadays with male sex.

In Central Park there is a meadow above the Ramble, a wooded area with winding paths which Frederick Law Olmsted and Calvert Vaux conceived of in 1858 as part of their general scheme to provide a sylvan environment ("pure and wholesome air, to act through the lungs") away from the jumble of the city—there is a meadow brim-full of men.

Men lounging bare-legged in little short shorts. Men lolling bare-chested in teeny bikinis. Men rubbing cocoa-butter lotion on each others' broad backs. Below the meadow, in the Ramble, men prowl—not so genteelly as Olmsted and Vaux might have intended, but certainly securing, as they professed, "an antithesis of objects of vision to those of the streets and houses, which should act remedially by impressions on the mind and suggestions to the imagination."

Out on the sand at Fire Island, men men men—and an occasional bare-breasted woman—lie face up on beach blankets. It is like "The Raft of the Medusa." Out in the surf heads bob above waves and shoulders wreathed with swimming suits. Rafts float farther out, nothing visible on them but limbs, intertwined.

And it's *worse* in the winter. To enter almost any popular gay bar in town on a weekend winter night after eleven—it is to be buffeted on all sides by flight-jacketed men—like being half-smothered by soft leather cushions, the kind you find in expensive cars. All that beefcake. All those men. Looking at, looking for each other.

Two blocks away from where I write this, there are no fewer than four gay bars—one Western-leather, one Hispano-Disco, one Frat-Mixer, one Deco-Decadent. To say nothing of the restaurants. (To say nothing of the waiters.)

So what am I doing inside? Am I the only one?

It is possible in my neighborhood to come up out of the subway from work and never make it home. It is possible in either of the two parks that flank my neighborhood to suck a hundred cocks in one night—or *two* hundred, for all *I* know. It is possible to take a short bus ride from my neighborhood and walk into another gay bar in another part of town, into another crowd, and not see one single man you have ever seen before in your life. *Anything* is possible.

You can get whipped and beaten by any one of thousands of considerate and obliging Masters. You can whip and beat any one of the many more thousands of willful and dedicated Slaves. You can get pissed on (and piss on), get fist-fucked (and fist-fuck), get your nipples pierced (and even your penis). You can have surgical needles driven into the palms of your hands. You can be hung upside down with a leather mask zipped over your head all Memorial Day weekend. You can get gang-banged in the back room of the International Stud, in the Mineshaft, in the Glory Hole, in countless other back-room bars. You can get banged and banged and never have to catch a single glimpse of a single face on any one of the men who so politely and efficiently service you in the utter darkness.

In other words, you can find romance.

The lovers. How do they do it? You see them, scads of them, sitting on their tartan car rugs, sipping chilled white wine, eating chicken tarragon, holding hands, listening to the New York Philharmonic under the stars. Roaming (a "decent" distance between them) through the Metropolitan Museum. Making goo-goo eyes at each other on the subway. Thousands of them. Two by two. How do they do it? Only a few of those pairs exhibit signs of patent psychosis. Only a few of them are so gauche as to slug it out in public. Only a few of them ask you to come home for a threesome—and when you get there it's like being entertained by Mr. and Mrs. Aristotle Onassis. The thousands of them you never even see! Burrowed away there in the cliffs of Manhattan, in Brooklyn brownstones, in Chelsea basements—a secret army of lovers. The only real marriages left in New York.

Am I the only one?

Now I'm sure that among the body count I'm so reluctant to take—leafing back through the pages of my journal (where *everything* has been written down, to make it more real), rifling my memory—there are more than a few limp dicks and excuses. But really. Am I the only one?

&

Sunday. My actor friend and I go for a walk in the park, down by the lake. When he turns to cross the bridge, I steer him away. I know he wants to stroll through the Ramble and that we will end up in the gay meadow. Not today. I can't take it.

"Why not?" he asks.

"Makes me nervous," I say, taking his arm and directing us toward the large, rowdy crowd clustered around a steel band.

He stops to toss a Frisbee back into the arms of a little kid.

"Not even just to watch?" he asks, his face a bit flushed from leaning down over the Frisbee.

"Not even just to watch," I say irritably. His aura of healthy sexuality is getting on my nerves. It is summer. He is tan. I am not. It's as good a reason as any for being cross at him. I put my hands in my pockets and walk on.

"The park was your idea," he says, catching up with me. "We really have to have a heart-to-heart, Danny," he says, putting an arm over my shoulder. "It's been too long."

I hunch down into the circle of his arm. "I'm going into sex therapy," I say.

"Good," he says. "You've become the most paranoid. . . ." He obviously thinks I'm joking.

But then he stops short, tugging at my neck in the process.

"What?"

"I'm going into sex therapy."

He smirks. He whistles. He wags his head a few times. He bites his tongue.

"Stop making faces."

"S-E-X. Sex therapy," he says.

"Yes."

"Good." He nods his head.

"I'm going into sex therapy."

"So what do you want me to say, Danny? I think it's terrific. When do you start?"

"I thought you were going to laugh at me."

He shrugs his shoulders, as if to admit the possibility, but he takes my arm again and we walk a few paces.

"Isn't it illegal?" he says.

"What do you mean?"

"I mean if money's changing hands."

"I'll pay Virgil. As usual."

"That's what I mean. Pandering? Surrogates?"

"It won't be with a surrogate," I say, as if surrogates were only for the fat, old and ugly. "It'll be with a partner."

He stares at me rather cross-eyed.

I explain. "Someone with the same problem."

"A slow cummer," he says.

"Yeah."

We walk on.

"Well," he says after a while, then sighs.

"I thought you'd laugh at me," I say again.

"You seem to be a bit disappointed in me," he says carefully, "as if you wanted me to talk you—"

But I've begun to cry.

"No no no no no," he says vehemently, once he has me sitting on a bench.

"I just need—some relief from this," I say, wiping my eyes with the back of my hand.

"Oh, Danny," he says, letting his hand rest on my shoulder, stroking my hair with the other. "Of course you do." Stares from passersby. "I've been so worried about you. Going through this alone. But now you'll have company!"

"Yeah," I sniffle. "Me and my 'partner.' Tandem ride off into the sunset."

We laugh.

"Oh, Danny," he says, sitting back on the bench, rubbing my shoulder. "I'm just glad I have a lover."

A

A lover. How ironic. Since I have every reason to believe that's how it all started.

You've heard the expression "go Hollywood"? Labelle used to sing about it: "Can I speak to you before you go Hollywood?" Meaning, can I talk to you without your attitude?

Well, one fall Max went to L.A. on business and "went Hollywood" besides. Oh, he came home. But essentially, Max was "in Hollywood" even when he was in New York with me.

Money and fame. The old story.

A classic passive-aggressive type, Max asked, when I said I was leaving, "What do you want me to do?" For two years he had been asking that.

"Nothing," I said. "Just let me out of here."

During my last six months with Max, I had cum two or three times the dozen or so times we actually got around to having sex. Max's mind was on money and fame, I guess. I don't know where mine was. On Max's money and fame, I suppose.

Well, anyone, however wrongheadedly monogamous he may have been, can learn all over again how to cruise, seduce, sparkle and shine. (Sing out, Louise!) The obligatory period of mourning slid into the obligatory period of fucking and sucking—but there was one problem I'd never had before.

With each new trick—however sparkling, however seductive I'd been, however hard, however wired—the body refused to perform.

♠

"I don't mean to be, um, uncharitable," my feminist friend once said. "But why this primacy of the orgasm?"

"*You'd* die if you couldn't cum," I pointed out.

Focused on her argument, she chose to ignore the personal reference, probed on. "It seems to amount to an obsession with you men, doesn't it? Now, if you couldn't get it up, Danny. . . . But you can. And yet you don't call it real sex unless you can cum every time, do you? It's just so typically male."

"What do you want?" I asked. "Reparations?" (She'd once allowed me to pay the check under that general rubric.)

"For all the women who've ever had to fake it?" She smiled wryly and shrugged. "Maybe. I'm not attacking you. It's just that I'll never understand why it's *so* important."

Oh, yes. There are certain slogans, all of them quite apt in themselves: "It isn't the destination, but the journey." "It isn't how big it is, but how you use it." "Pick yourself up, dust yourself off, and start all over again."

But it *is* very important. Why? I don't know. But it is. Isn't it?

♠

Max taught me to hate gay men. I realized that early on, after we broke up, when I'd been seeing my new shrink, Virgil, for some few weeks.

"I hate 'em," I said. "They're out to get me."

"What do they want from you?" he asked.

"I don't know. But I'm not going to give it to them."

A

Up and down Christopher Street. A bitterly cold night, the first night I've ventured OUT after Max. I'm very drunk and very aware of what it's done to me—brought my bitterness and longing into bold relief. The two emotions pinwheel in me. I'm what the shrinks would call "in conflict"—a sincerely confused but nevertheless (from my viewpoint) rather reprehensible state.

I make the rounds. . . .

Too cold for cruising clothes. ("One always," says my political friend, "sacrifices function for identification." And thus my flimsy jacket doesn't cover my cold buns.) Too cold ever to warm up, even standing in a small room with a hundred men. Too cold ever to forget the cold. Every face is tight with it.

Standing in the Ramrod, finally, I order a shot of Scotch. It takes off the chill a bit and my teeth stop chattering. Of all the places I've been tonight—and I've hit them all—this is the most cheerful. Relatively. Only leathermen, it seems (for this is a leather bar), so elaborately macho in their imposing getups, can afford to be friendly without risking their souls. ("The very last bastion of personality," says my novelist friend. "In an increasingly artificial subculture, *their* fantasy selves are intact, so they can *be* themselves when they choose.") One of them steps up beside me at the bar, to order a drink.

Tall, carapaced in black leather from the tips of his boots to his lean jaw, head shaved, with a mustache that would do a yeoman of the guard proud, he leans up against the bar and quite candidly gives me the once-over. Whether his interest is a statement on my outré outfit or on my sex appeal, I don't know.

He extends a big, fleshy hand. The other, holding a beer, is gloved.

I shake his hand and we exchange names. He is easily six inches taller than I, and has to stoop down to hear my replies to his unceasing questions. No problem making conversation with *him*, as any remark suffices to keep him rolling. Finally, I confine myself to a series of grunts and yeahs while he tells me about his summer in Italy—don't ask me how he got on that.

I've been like a vat of molten bile all evening. At Ty's, I sneered at the tourists. ("Bridge and tunnel boys," my Fire Island friend calls them, the boys from New Jersey and the outer boroughs who invade Christopher Street every weekend.) At Julius, I sneered at the young professionals dressed in the same button-down shirts and crew-neck sweaters they sported back in the Ivy League. ("Office queens with no sense of rhythm whatsoever, but heavenly husband material," my dancing friend says of them.) At the Eagle, I sneered at the strutting old leather queens as they chatted about the Bloomingdale's white sale. ("Your double standard about sex is hilarious sometimes," says my feminist friend. "A *real* man obviously can't be interested in designer sheets and still be good sex.")

I've been all evening like a pool of poison. ("It's interesting," says my actor friend. "Lately when you think you're being hostile, you're not half as hostile as when you think you're being nice.") I don't know if the man at my side perceives it. He *has* been the first to dare to approach me this evening. . . .

I am very grateful, but don't let on.

"Time to go," he says finally, setting down the empty beer can and taking a black glove out from under an epaulet, but not otherwise shifting his stance. His free hand comes to rest on the crown of my ass. He peers down at me, his eyes somewhat hooded by the overhead light. "Wanna get it on?"

"I don't know," I say, surprised by his invitation and even more grateful than before for his attention.

"I don't live far," he says. "Cold out. . . ."

He is not enticing me, just stating cases. I think of the icy trek to Sheridan Square, the numbed trip uptown on the subway.

"What's," I stammer, "what's expected of me?" Which

one of us gets strung up, which one of us whipped? The way I'm feeling tonight, for his sake it had better be me. The glint in his eye, let alone the discrepancy between our heights, seems to promise it *will* be me.

He purses his lips. "Well, tonight. . . ." His dark eyes look amused. "Tonight . . . I just saw *Tosca*, and to tell the truth, I'm feeling mellowed out. You?"

I do not say, I want to be strung up, whipped and loved.

No, I say, "I just left my lover and I'm fucked up."

"Oh, little boy," he says, shaking his head, "don't ever say that. . . ." He straightens up, shakes my hand, and leaves.

Walking back up Christopher Street, with the freezing wind slapping me like wet rags, I rehearse my new litany about gay men, whom I've learned to hate. How I hate them. How I hate myself. How I hate Virgil, my new shrink, for not curing me of the perfidious Max before throwing me into this inhuman mess.

▲

Remember the dentist, Danny?

Oh, yeah. Him. Well, you see, it was clear *that* relationship was on the skids.

But he belonged to your political friend, Danny.

I was drunk.

But you stole him right out from under your friend's nose.

He was in the middle of a divorce. I suppose I took advantage of his confusion, yeah.

How many times did you see him?

Oh, who knows.

And how did it end?

Look, it was plain as could be that he wanted a husband, to replace his wife.

But how?

I—ah—stopped returning his calls.

And why?

Well, he wanted to get married. I wasn't ready for that.

Oh?

I despised him. All right?
But why?
He was too nice.
And?
I couldn't cum.

▲

My trusty *Joy of Gay Sex* (for all the good it's done me)
tells me that a "late comer" like me "exercises such tight
control over his feelings as well as his body that he avoids
anxiety but may suffer from such displacements of anxiety
as an upset stomach or a tendency to skin rash."
    My stomach aches. I learned long ago what this means:
I am unhappy. But new symptoms accompany it: my balls,
my cock, the muscles between my legs ache. My asshole
aches. The pain is fierce, cramps coming in waves.
    It's because I'm going to meet *him* tonight. My "part-
ner."
    All Virgil would tell me about "Joe" is that he is Italian
(the Italian Stallion!), twenty-six, and "not what I believe
you call a troll."

▲

Joe is not a troll. He is a nice-looking guy, about six feet
tall, warm brown eyes, a head of thick brown-black hair,
slender (great forearms), nicely dressed in "the uniform" (I,
too, wore flannel shirt and jeans tonight) and sunburned
from last weekend at the beach.
    He lives with his parents in Massapequa, Long Island.
He sells men's clothes at the local Korvettes. He is, I
gathered from our "getting to know you" conversation over
coffee after meeting at Virgil's, drifting.
    In Virgil's office, he was twitching and blushing with
anxiety. He could barely answer Virgil's innocuous questions. I felt like screaming at him: Relax!

I was cool as the proverbial cucumber. The cramps had abated somewhat.

But, oh, Joe's problems. The ambiguous relationship with a woman that ended badly about a year ago. The queens at his local bar, a typically tight-knit little circle where everyone knows who you've slept with and when—and Joe hasn't. His parents, who don't know he's gay or why he's gone into group therapy at the local mental health center. (The woman friend evidently tried to kill herself—perhaps over Joe—he is unclear about it, guilty.) Joe's aimlessness. Not cumming.

I know I'm no prize, but Joe's problems, as he sat across from me in the coffee shop, laying them out, or letting me drag them out. . . . Joe's problems seemed to magnify my own. And while learning about Joe's anxieties made me feel "healthy" by comparison (so Virgil's group therapy *has* done me some good), my own anxiety about doing this has increased. If we *do* go through with this, how much do I have to deal with Joe's problems, too?

If we do go through with this. What is *this*?

A

"You know, of course," said Virgil. "This matchmaking, this creating couples. It's hardly scientific. You have to decide for yourselves."

I looked at Joe. He was looking out the window. I looked away, and I became aware as Virgil was talking that Joe was now looking at *me*. We were checking each other out the way you check out people in a bar, and allowing each other to do it, each as if unaware that one was checking out the other. . . . I smiled to myself.

Joe is not a troll. What he is, is an entirely different person.

We have one week to decide.

A

What is so frightening is the prospect of intimacy. I've been thinking about how for Joe and me sex is synonymous not with physical release but with this frightening intimacy. How somewhere along the line cumming became the final sign of accepting that intimacy. How for us sex is full of static, like a busted radio.

⚑

Virgil asks for our decision. Blushing, tentative, virginal and shy as we seldom are in "real life," we agree to try.

⚑

A weekend in the Pines with my Fire Island friend. So near to Joe but so far away—light years away from the disco where Joe and his friends dance, wearing the same clothes we wear, dancing to the same music, getting off on it as we do.

And here I am in Disneyland. My last fling. Once Joe and I begin therapy, we can't have sex with anyone else. Virgil says it only "reinforces bad habits."

Joe seldom goes to the City, has never been to the Island, looked rather stricken and envious when I told him I was coming out here this weekend.

⚑

My friend has taken this house for many summers running. I love this house because it reminds me of my parents' house—the Melmac dinnerware in the corner hutch, for instance; the homely stabs at decorating, everything color-coordinated shades of green; the fact that all this was done for the Summer People by someone who was obviously not gay.

"I always *intend* to do something with it," says my Fire Island friend, surveying the living room, with its gaudy calypso-dancer prints and plastic swag lamps. "But I never get around to it."

"Body bags," says my dancing friend immediately. He has dropped by for a drink; he lives with a covey of decorators at the other end of the Pines, in a house he calls "Interiors City." "Body bags! Plastic body bags. We'll just zip up everything! The couch, the basket chairs, that dreadful table. . . ."

This mordant or misplaced humor is as much a fixture of the Island as are the dunes themselves—as if so much profound physical beauty (both the beauty of the landscape and the beauty of the many Beauties who flock here) must be offset by an equally tenacious mockery.

The house sits atop the spine of the Island. It is undistinguished (a tract house, really) but for its placement: its spectacular view of the Atlantic through the floor-to-ceiling windows in the living room, its view of the shallow bay from the kitchen. It has two bedrooms, one large bedroom for my friend and a smaller bedroom, which he ushers me into and calls "the Princess Suite," painted yellow, with dimity curtains.

It is a quiet house, separated from its neighbors on the bay side by an acreage of foliage—deer rustle through the undergrowth in the mornings. Common-sense domesticity seems to rule this end of the Pines, remote as it is from the gaudier showplaces along Ocean Walk, huge monstrosities with batten-board battlements that remind me of the tin Prince Valiant Brand castle I played with as a child. From where I stand, as a matter of fact, out on the front deck, with the boom of the breakers caressing my ears, the tiny figures to the south, standing on the parapets and lounging under snapping pennants on the decks, look very much like the miniature knights in armor I used to deploy across the kitchen floor. Oiled chests (so assiduously built up in that final, impressive effort at the gym, lest summer catch them unawares) reflect the glow of the setting sun.

My last fling. But the very distance between me and

those bodies is already curiously satisfying. I realize that not being able to trick will be a blessing not so ill-disguised.

The moon appears in the sky like the crescent-shaped mark left on sunburned flesh after you press it with your finger. Everything is vivid out here, and distinct. The sun, masked by wisps of clouds laid out across the sky like cheese-cloth, seems to skid down toward the horizon, like a bucket attached to a line, tugged through the water by a wader digging for clams. . . .

I sigh deeply. This is what I've come for. Not the men.

Not that I don't feel a certain obligation. . . .

After all, it will be the last time. For some time. For—who knows *how* long?

Gossip over my shoulder inside the house. My dancing friend has just disclosed that Jim Stockton (whoever *he* is) is dating a Spanish-Lebanese editor of something called the *International Maritime Diary.* "Halvah with *salsa picante?*" asks my Fire Island friend.

"Hair for days," says my dancing friend.

▲

One A.M. My Fire Island friend pleads exhaustion, then changes his mind, gets dressed—then falls asleep half on, half off his bed, feet on the floor, where he was resting while I chose among the five or six T-shirts I've brought out here for dancing. I don't attempt to wake him up, slip out of the house, and walk down to the Sandpiper alone.

The place is jammed. No one *I* know. This is my fourth visit to Fire Island—if you count the wretched week I spent alone a couple of years ago, in the Grove, in a two-by-four rented room. *That* was another Fire Island altogether. What I chiefly remember about it, besides how much it cost me of my almost nonexistent weekly salary, was that I was never out of earshot of the sound of music all that long week spent alone. It was disco, disco, disco—morning, noon, and through the sleepless night. As my dancing friend often says, disco should stay *in* the disco; it should not be allowed to follow us into "real life."

How kind my Fire Island friend is! To have invited me out here. Not a munificent gesture from his point of view. He says he could use the company—his house is *very* quiet. But can he appreciate how huge his generosity seems to me now? As I mount the steps to the Sandpiper? Knowing I have a home to return to and that I don't have to scour the beach and the meat rack at five in the morning for "accommodations" like some of the daytrippers dancing here at the Sandpiper right now?

No. It can't be. Surprisingly enough, I *do* know someone here. Out of the crush of bodies on the dance floor dances—my political friend. The last time I saw *him*, we were marching up Fifth Avenue on Gay Pride Day. He had a lavender carnation behind his ear.

Not tonight. Tonight he wears lemon-colored painter's pants and a shocking-pink athletic shirt, a plastic belt and blue suede dancing shoes. (Wherever did he get them?) I note, however, that he has topped off this extraordinary (for him) costume with a thin chain around his neck, from which depends a small silver lambda, symbol of gay pride.

"What are *you* doing here?" he gasps, out of breath from his exertions. He is literally dripping with sweat. His hot, skinny arm snakes around my waist.

"And *you*?" I say.

"Don't you just *adore* it out here? Isn't this what a gay world would look like? Isn't this what a gay world would *feel* like? Of course it isn't *perfect*, but it's as close to a gay utopia as anything there is, isn't it?"

I wonder why he is straining so hard to justify something that for me seems on the order of a force of nature, the Island.

"Don't you want to dance?" he asks, his narrow hip bumping against mine.

"Not yet," I say, sure that I'm still a bit too sober to absorb the spectacle of my political friend consorting so enthusiastically with the very milieu he's always seemed to resent so—as exemplifying all the ills of gay life: ingrown, artificial, hedonistic, uncharitable, moneyed. But I keep my thoughts to myself. I'm not one to talk about enemies-in-our-midst or to cast stones; not I, who learned after Max to hate gay men.

Max. Of course. The last time I was here it was with Max.

After a few more attempts to get me out onto the dance floor, my political friend disappears with a wave of his hand into the gyrating revelers. I push my way through the crowd and pick up a drink, push my way back and out onto the deck, walk up the stairs to the rooftop deck. Less populated.

Perched on a canvas folding chair, glowing in the shadows like twin ghosts, sits a pair of white shoes. I take them off the chair and sit down, placing them on the deck beside me.

"Those are mine," a voice intones from the darkness at the end of the deck.

"Sorry," I say, as if the chair were, of course, the personal property of this stranger—so potent are the unwritten Laws of the Island.

"That's all right," he says. His bald head gleams in the moonlight.

I take a sip of my drink.

"Lovely evening," the bald man says.

"Yes," I say.

"So mild."

"Yes."

"Hot as hell in the city."

"Yes." (Wondering how he can pack such innocuous remarks so full of insinuation. . . .)

"First time out this year?" he asks.

"Uh—yes, it is."

"You need some color," he says.

I look down at my pale arms, paleness accentuated by my dark blue T-shirt—a poor choice from among five or six poor choices.

I'm not ready! a voice screams inside me.

Your last fling, a smaller voice whispers next to my ear.

"Staying in the Pines?" the bald man asks.

"Yes," I say.

"You don't recognize me, do you?"

"Well, I wasn't sure," I lie, peering into the shadows.

"I shaved my head."

"Oh."

"Yep. Just shaved it off. What was left."

"It's—very flattering," I say.

"You still don't recognize me."

"No. No, I don't."

"Some people find bald heads very exciting. Sexually," he says.

"I don't know," I say, spine stiffening. He is a well-mannered troll, of course. But he is fast turning into a toad. A toad, as my Fire Island friend would say, fast on his way to becoming a full-fledged dragon.

"I'm only asking for your opinion," he says.

"I've never thought about it," I lie.

Then I realize who he is.

No. It can't be. But could it possibly? Max's agent? The nice man who had us out here that summer? Max's agent? Who I liked so much? It *can't* be Max's agent. Coming on to me like this. . . .

I jerk myself out of the chair and stand there shivering for a moment, as if the temperature on the deck has just abruptly dropped fifty degrees or so.

"What's wrong?"

I mumble something, but I am already walking away rapidly, down the stairs, down the steps, down the boardwalk, away from the Sandpiper.

&

What am I doing in the meat rack?

Cursing Max, cursing Max's agent, cursing myself, I lurch into the shrubbery at the foot of the boardwalk.

Branches whip back as I pass. Then I pause. Catch my breath.

The stillness of the leaves is magnified by the darkness and the silence. The rapid beating of my heart has replaced the tattoo of my feet on the boardwalk, fleeing Max's agent, fleeing Max's ghost, fleeing the Sandpiper, like Lillian Gish in *Way Down East,* leaving civilization behind. . . .

Well, almost. Strokes of white paint blaze the twisting paths. Somebody charitably has marked the trees to light our way. I've come all the way to the Grove.

Walking to the wrong side of a sapling, I find myself in the underbrush.

A wide plank gleams in the moonlight. Taking it for a way out (and wondering why the fuck I ever came in here in the first place—*Your last fling,* a voice insists), I step onto the plank. It sinks into the swamp, taking my foot with it.

And ruining my dancing pumps.

I struggle to the top of the bank and stand between two—elms? There is no sound at all. Not even the sound of the ocean, so near. I turn to look around. *No one's here,* sighs another voice, with relief. But I know better. It's never too early or too late for the meat rack. . . .

There's a break in the crown of shrubs on the ridge of the dune. I go through it, descend into a clearing. Light a cigarette. (*Join Smokenders, join Smokenders,* chides the Gishy voice.) Inhale. . . .

Well, here you are. After all. (Voice of normality.) *Where safer to exhibit your dysfunction?* ("Sorry, man," I hear myself saying to some genuflecting supplicant. "I just came three times.") *It's so fucking dark.* . . .

And you are horny. After all. (That underlying sibilance; he's disguised his voice, but it's old Scratch, the Tacky Tempter himself. Perhaps this is something like the trials of Job, and God is testing me not with boils but with a very modern curse, not cumming. . . .)

Aha. At the edge of another clearing, a man sits on a

clump of grass, beneath a black tropical-looking tree. The path curves around him into the woods.

I sit down beside him.

It's a trap! screams the voice of Lillian Gish. *It's a golden opportunity*, counsels the Apostate Angel, this time in the voice of W. C. Fields.

He takes my hand.

"Hello," I say.

Adorable, young, fresh-faced, he shakes his head. Primed for rejection, I begin to stand up. But he pulls me down, points to his ears, each in turn.

"Ah," I mime. "I see. No hear." (*He isn't an idiot, for christsake*, says the voice of reason. *He's deaf.*)

Well, that certainly cuts down on the dreary preliminaries. I kiss him, and he returns the kiss, and then, so suddenly it leaves my mouth agape, he pulls away.

He's been spooked by seeing another man passing, disappearing into a low opening in the woods.

The deaf man has not released my hand, but is strangely—diffident? His face is so fresh, his mien so—otherworldly.

Hast thou not dropp'd from heaven?

It's William Shakespeare. I'd know those clipped, fruity accents anywhere.

Out o' the moon, I do assure thee—blabbing lines out of *The Tempest*.

I caress his cheek, run three fingers down the side of his throat, wonder if he can speak. He smiles. I kiss him again, just lightly. He doesn't pull back this time, grasps my knee. I kiss him again, then the hand floats up to my chest, urges me away. . . .

Why? Who is he waiting for? Why can't it be me?

We sit sharing a cigarette, then I duck into the woods through a low passageway.

That wasn't so bad, now, was it, Danny? my friend Bill says. *And just look at that moon*, he gushes.

I'm hungry, grumbles Ms. Gish.

Hey, Danny, look at that! shrieks Beelzebub.

It's nothing. Just an ordinary blowjob, shrugs the voice of sanity.

Shut up, I tell them all. The secret, of course, is not to think. Don't try to remember the rest of that speech from *The Tempest,* for instance. . . . *I was the man i' the moon, when time was . . .da-da da-da, something else, something else. . . .* Willie falters.

Walking through the alleyways, chutes and causeways worn into the thickest part of the woods, I pass dozens of men now. I can barely make out their features. In any case, they pall beside my memory of the deaf man, and I wonder again what, who, he is waiting for—and what *I'm* looking for, having left him behind.

Abruptly then, I turn into a corner alcove and find it occupied almost solely, it seems at first, by a magnificent torso, fluorescent, clad in white. The arms are almost as dark as the foliage behind. The face is in utter darkness. It is Roman armor in Dayglo.

I slip my arms around the statue, and his face, now too close for me to see anyway, moves in on mine. Our arms lock around each other.

CONTACT!

We kiss. Deep. Deep. But on the very edge of the kiss, as it becomes inevitable that it must go either deeper yet or diminish (and I feel his hardon against my leg, return the pressure with mine against his), he bites me. Once, twice, like a snake striking.

I give out a little squeal. This is not a turn-on for me. I push him away, but he holds my shoulders and pulls me back. I jerk away, and his hands trail off lightly, along my shoulders, along my arms. I plunge into the woods.

Run, Lillian, run.

I feel like Bambi with the forest fire at my back.

Now I am definitely walking in circles, trying to get the fuck out of here. I pass the deaf man again, his moon face turned to the heavens. . . .

I do adore thee . . .I will kiss thy foot . . .I prithee. . . .

Heads turn to follow my ragged progress through the woods. I stop to light another cigarette.

To my left, there is a wet sound, a swampy sound, like the sound my shoe made when I pulled it out of the muck.

I look around and down. A huge, hairy man lies on his back in the undergrowth. He is completely naked, his clothes hanging on the branch of a shrub next to him. But he *is* wearing glasses—black frames and heavy lenses. A can of Crisco sits at his side. (He has ever given new meaning for me to the Boy Scout slogan.) A bluish pool of semen rests on his belly.

A boy not more than sixteen kneels between his outstretched legs. The legs are descending to the bracken, like two white dirigibles. The boy is licking a wet fist.

They both look up at me and smile beatifically.

"Hi," I say, all Miss Congeniality. "Does either of you know the way out of here?"

The hairy man wearily lifts a pale hand and points out the exit.

I pull myself up onto the boardwalk and stumble into the shadows, and right into the arms of—

My dancing friend holds me up by the belt.

"What are *you* doing here?"

"My last fling," I say meekly.

A

"You're hardly a meat-rack person, Danny," says my actor friend the next day on the beach. We are lying on an old sheet he's dragged out here, printed with likenesses of Raggedy Ann and Raggedy Andy. My actor friend is utterly disingenuous about the sheet. I speculate to myself that cartoon sheets are liable to be all the rage in a matter of weeks; that's how these things catch on.

His lover lies beside him, with his nose buried in a copy of *Bleak House*, from which he has not emerged since we tripped down onto the sand.

In spite of all their admonitions, I am getting burned.

The two of *them* are the color of teak, and darkening as we talk.

"Why ever did you drag yourself down *there?*" my actor friend asks.

I eye the copy of *Bleak House* covetously. "I don't know. I guess I had something to prove to myself."

"Well, I've always said that of all the faggots I know," my actor friend says, adjusting his inflatable pillow, "Danny's the *only* one I know who needs a diamond solitaire on his pinkie before he'll go all the way. The meat rack indeed."

"It's my last chance," I say, scanning the beach, like Ahab on the lookout for Moby Dick—completely convinced, of course, that dick is the name of the game. I am aware of a slightly metallic taste in my mouth. My mouth is dry with sexual panic and unrequited lust.

My friend's lover sets down his book, carefully marking his place, and scrambles to his feet. "I think I'll take a walk," he says, leaning down and giving his lover a kiss on the cheek.

"Have a good time," my actor friend says, not in the slightest dismayed by this ritual. His lover is walking now in the direction of the meat rack, and we both know he will not emerge from there until time for Tea Dance.

With a sigh, I fall back on my towel. They've been together—what is it?—ten years last Fourth of July, their arbitrary anniversary. I think of Max (not far from my mind, I assure you, since last night) and how, if I'd had the balls or the native wit, I would have kept him on a leash out here. As it was, of course, he seldom strayed from my side; we were both that unsure about ourselves. . . .

"Hon-ey," my actor friend coos under his breath. A statuesque model-type saunters by at the edge of the surf. "That number," my friend says, when the model is out of earshot. "I see that number at Georgette Klinger all the time."

"Not my type," I say, contemplating a facial myself. I'll need one after this barbecue.

"What type is Joe? Joe's the name, right?"

"Tall. Italian. Young. Shy."
"Smack-smack."
"He's nice."
"Just my type exactly," he says.
"What am I going to do?" I ask.
"Relax."

▲

Saturday night. The Ice Palace. My Fire Island friend pops half a Quaalude into my mouth.
"Relax," he says.
"What will it do to me?" I gasp.
"Relax you. It's a hypnotic. Geared for endurance dancing. Come on. It'll kick in on its own. You won't even notice." He grabs my arm and drags me out onto the dance floor. The place is as packed as a Tokyo rush hour.

The cocaine he shoved up my nose before we came out has given me an advanced case of sinusitis. And an awful taste in the back of my mouth uncannily like unrequited lust. As for sexual panic, it has accelerated through Tea Dance and now through this to Indy 500 velocity.

"It's a very nice high," my dancing friend said of the cocaine, looking on approvingly as I sniffed the white dust from the matchstick my Fire Island friend held under my quivering nostril. I sneezed, like the tyro I am. "Like champagne," said my dancing friend. And he was right. But now, three hours later and cruising into dawn, my Fire Island friend has decided it's time to "contour our drugs"—and thus the Quaalude.

My jeans hang, soggy, off my hips. I'm sure if I could hear them—but who can hear *anything* over the music in here?—my shoes would squish, just as they did on the way home from the meat rack last night.

To the lush strains of Donna's "MacArthur Park," which seems to have been playing for an eternity now, my Fire Island friend and I dance. I try to ignore the sappy lyrics. Not too difficult. All I hear is the pounding in my head. I turn around, bumping, with my ass to him, and he places his hands on my hips, moves them to and fro, twists them back and forth. We dance like two adolescent orangutans in heat—"mounting behavior," as the zoologists would say. This is the only sexual byplay we've allowed ourselves for months—after the time we went to bed and I, of course, "failed" with him. . . .

I move back into him, and his arms slide up my sides, his hands clasp in front of me, at the solar plexus, his hot breath blows past my ear.

"Ohhhh mahgawd," I say.

"It's the Quaalude," he shouts in my ear. He runs fingernails across my ribs.

"Ohhhh mahgawd."

"Sensitive?"

"Ohhhh mahgawd."

▲

Dawn. We walk back along the beach from the Grove to the Pines. My arm is flung over his shoulders.

"If you'd just look around you, Danny," he is saying. "That guy cruised you until he went cross-eyed."

"He was looking at you," I say.

"No he wasn't. He was looking at you. He was drilling holes through you."

"I *saw* him." I stumble in the sand and hold him tighter. "I wasn't interested. Anyway, *you're* the one who made me take off my glasses."

"Get contacts," he says. "And would you *please* do something about your hair?" He ruffles my disheveled hair. He's right; it's too long for the disco.

I believe my Fire Island friend really thinks I am coming along just fine since I fell under his patronage. And he is right. Since I met him, I have coincidentally unlearned how to hate gay men.

We stagger up the steps and onto Ocean Walk. I stop to

tie my shoelace. "Don't stop," he says. "You'll never get started again."

"Look at the sun," I say. "It's just like *West Side Story.*"

"And don't look at the sun. It's dangerous this low." He urges me on, his arm around my waist.

A cardinal pipes from the shrubbery and my friend answers it. Our feet thud softly along the boardwalk. He carries on a dialogue with the bird until its cry diminishes and dies.

I pine for one to whom I can speak my FIRST THOUGHTS, dear Henry Thoreau says inside my head. *One to whom I can be transparent instinctively,* he sighs. *Like cuttle fish we conceal ourselves. . . .*

"Did you know he came here looking for Margaret Fuller's bones? When she drowned off this island?"

"Who?" my friend asks.

"Henry David Thoreau."

"Oh."

"It's a very Thoreauvian sunrise, isn't it? He never found them."

"What?"

"Margaret Fuller's bones. . . ."

At home, we fall into his bed—our dancing friend has been displaced from his own house into the Princess Suite, in deference to a new arrival at Interiors City.

"Do you always sleep in your underwear?" I say, patting my friend's butt, the damp shorts.

"No." His face is turned away from me, into the pillow.

"Thank you for a lovely evening," I say, very June Allyson for some reason. I let my hand stay where it is.

And my Fire Island friend, who has so generously taken me into his house, fed me, drugged me—he takes me in his arms, and the "problem" is no longer a problem. . . .

Almost.

When we are sixty-five, Joe
and I joke, we will be running ads in the personals:

Older Gentleman
Fit and Willing
Wants Younger Gentleman Willing to
SHOWER AND TALC
No Fats, Fems, Dopesters, Bikers
Good Clean Fun

For we have been showering and talcing twice a week for
three weeks now. (Virgil calls it the Prune Stage.) We are
very clean.

First we soap each other thoroughly in the shower and
rinse. Then we get out and dry each other. Finally, we talc.
We are forbidden to go beyond this. We report our feelings,
fantasies, thoughts in detail to Virgil—as we will do with all
our exercises in the months (months?) to come. The sensa-
tions in each part of the exercise are very different.

Joe and I call this state "desensitization." (Virgil himself
dispenses no cant.) I have ceased to look upon Joe as a sex
object. The first time we stepped into the shower (at my

apartment, for obvious reasons) I had a raging hardon. Joe
was limp.

What fantasies I had! Joe shoving me up against the tile
wall, sticking his fingers up my butt, then fucking me while
the warm water beats down on our writhing bodies. Me
going down on Joe's engorged cock while he gargles his
delight under the relentless spray. Joe sucking my nipples,
one after the other, then reaching down to cup my balls in
his hand, tonguing the head of my dripping prick while the
water courses down my spine and eddies into my asshole.
What fantasies!

Joe says he had none.

Now I get hard only when Joe soaps or dries my cock.
We are shy of body contact—"Oh, excuse me"—and methodical about our tasks. I'm reminded of first-aid class,
where, after all, we were never required to *demonstrate*
mouth-to-mouth. . . .

My vanity has been sorely tried these past few weeks. I
want Joe to look at me, lust after me, compliment me as I loll
against the basin and he dusts my fine young body. He
doesn't. And *he*, he is very secretive, very private, wants no
compliments from me, no come-ons. He says they make him
nervous. He says he's going to be deliberately "selfish, in this
for myself." One night I complained to Virgil that Joe was
cold. Virgil encouraged me to "voice other fantasies."

Nevertheless, I privately think Joe *is* rather cold, disen-
gaged, distant. That's his way of coping with the demands of
the situation. Mine is to be the best student in the class; I'd
take notes in the shower if I could.

Shower and talc. Shower and talc.

We see Virgil for an hour or less each week. He is brisk
and businesslike, half shrink, half recreation director. He
tells us not to worry, though he knows we will. Every week
we report new anxieties—all over showering. One of our
major worries is that we will never, now that we've gotten to
know every nook and cranny of each others' bodies, never
get it up for sex. Yet, strangely, it is soothing, this twice-

weekly contact with a proper stranger. Since I know Joe doesn't want anything out of me (but for me to keep my distance right now), I'm already learning to relax more with him.

We have been instructed to talk a lot, say what feels good, what we don't like. And since the walls are thin in my apartment house, I often (while Joe is soaping my asshole, for instance, or even just my feet) wonder what my neighbors might think. This tall young man comes to my door with a little box of pastries or a shopping bag precisely at 8:00 P.M. At approximately eight-forty-five, the shower goes on. Muffled voices from the bathroom for about an hour. Then the nice-looking young man departs.

What are my favorite erogenous zones? I couldn't tell you. They've just about gone underground for the duration. I know what "feels nice." Joe has a swift, sure, efficient touch. As a matter of fact, both of us very well might be in training to be nurses rather than hot humpy numbers. . . .

Joe doesn't have stomach problems like me. He has acne.

Joe and I have agreed that neither of us is the other's type. That is, we would not cruise each other in a bar. Neither of us knows quite whether to be offended by this or not.

Shower and talc. Shower and talc.

⚠

"Mind lifting your foot?"
"What?"
"I said, would you mind lifting your foot."
"Why?"
"So I can wash it."
He lifts his foot. "You never do that foot first," he says.
"What do you mean?" I lather up his foot.
"You always do the right one first."
"That bother you?"

"Doing the right one first?" He braces himself against the tile wall.

"That I'm doing the left one. If, indeed, I always do the right one first."

"Look," he says, "I'm not making a big deal."

"Yes you are," I say. He is subterranean, but not *that* subterranean. I can tell.

"*You're* making a big deal," he says.

With a twist of the ankle, of course, I could quite easily bring him crashing to the bottom of the tub. "All right," I say, as if to drop it.

But he knows I won't, will bring it up later. Wishing to forestall that, he says, "No big deal."

I move up to his calf. This is his particular pleasure, after standing on his feet all day, but I skim over it and up to the kneecap.

"What about my calf?" he finally asks.

"What about it?"

"You just . . . ."

I move back down. "I don't want to be accused of being too mechanical," I say, nasty.

▲

"Look at that, will ya?"

"Yeah."

Joe is soaping my cock. "Hasn't done that for a long time," he says.

"No." My cock is sticking hard and red out of the suds.

He begins to hum to himself.

"I suppose you're going to say," he says, giving my cock a final dollop of lather, "that *I* did that."

"No. I wasn't."

"Since. . . ."

"Since what?"

He turns me around and begins on my ass.

"Since what?" I ask again.

"Since you always think I'm getting sexy with you."

"I don't always think that at all." His hand goes into the crack of my ass. "Do I?"

"I'm not."

"I know you're not. Sometimes I wish you would."

"Well, I'm not."

"You know," I say, "you're just like my old lover, Max."

"Thanks." He moves up to my back. Was that a pinch?

"A person has to be always reading you," I say. "You can't have *no* responses."

"I have responses."

"You never talk about them."

"I talk about them." He is angry now. I can feel it on my shoulders.

"*I* yank them out of you," I say.

Silence for a while.

"I'm not your lover Max," he says finally.

"No," I say. I've been thinking in the interim, while he's finishing my back. "But he was the last man I—was intimate with."

&

The men on the street are driving me crazy. Joe reports the same reaction to guys trying on clothes in Korvettes.

"But what if you run into the love of your life at the Cockring?" my actor friend asks.

"I don't know. Maybe I can get his phone number."

"But what will you say? 'I'm in sex therapy and can't sleep with you'?"

"God, no."

"Well you ought to think of something. Unless you're getting enough sex from what's-his-name as it is."

"Joe. And it isn't sex, for godsake. I told you."

"But what is it, then, if it isn't sex?"

&

Massage.

We are massaging now with baby oil. It's nice to be out of the shower, though we still shower together afterward. Joe philosophizes that massage is a bit like the multiplication tables. He says that eventually, you see, we'll work our way up to the dreaded trigonometry. But we should never forget addition and good old subtraction (shower and talc). Joe likes the showers. He attributes this to the fact that he's a water sign.

For the first time in years (to Joe's obvious delight; misery does love company) *my* skin is breaking out. All that fucking baby oil. It doesn't seem to matter how thoroughly Joe scrubs my back, and I wonder if I'm projecting his anxiety symptoms onto myself. . . .

Now, now. No analysis. Analysis is just another way of rendering this admittedly bizarre situation even more bizarre. . . .

At first we were forbidden to do nipples, asses, or cocks and balls. I'm still more excitable than Joe, and a few erogenous zones have resurfaced. But his intentions are so— well, so honorable. I finally believe that. He is not hiding all the responses that I find so easy to verbalize. He is just smothered in defenses. Given the aboveboard circumstances, it is impossible to maintain any sexual tension. What lesson can I learn from *that*? Mystery = lust?

I jack off before *and* after Joe's visits. But I never think of Joe. Should I? Is that normal? What *is* normal?

We're still supposed to talk a lot. Virgil has emphasized it. And there's more to talk about with massage. Much more sensual. I realize how little I used to talk in bed. Talking per se is not the issue, of course. Communicating our desires is—"Down a little farther on the left," etc. Everyone knows that, you're saying. Yeah, but I suppose this is one of the things Joe and I have to learn, or relearn. We've never had the opportunity with others. Perhaps because we haven't extended an invitation? Or is it the façade we wear, we men, into sexual situations?

When we report our sessions to Virgil, going over them

with a fine-tooth comb, it's like *Rashomon*—there are two versions of just about everything we do. (Who knows what *Virgil* thinks.) We are still edgy and suspicious of each other, avoiding that fearful intimacy, I guess. We've managed to do so fairly well. I realize that the fact we oil each other's assholes twice a week might tend to contradict that last statement. . . .

⚠

"What was he like?"
"He was the best roommate anyone could have."
"Come on."
"He was very quiet. Nice. Well-liked. Everyone liked him. My friends liked him."
"Your legs are real tight tonight."
"I walked home from work."
"And?"
"And what?"
"Max."
"I'd rather not talk about it."
Joe moves to my other leg, right on schedule.
"And you're always telling me . . ." he says.
"It's a long story," I say.
"What am I here for?"
"I was happier talking about fall fashions."
Joe sighs and kneads my calf. His hands are warm and slippery. Idly, I watch his cock bobbing back and forth between his legs. I watch his stomach contracting and relaxing in time to his movements. I watch his pectoral muscles moving under the smooth skin. I see he is looking directly into my eyes.
"You're very sexy," I say impulsively.
He blinks, looks down at my leg, works it.
"I'm not?" I say. "What am I? Chopped liver?" A joke. But not quite.
"You're . . .cute."

"Cute."

"Yeah," he says, as one would say to a playful puppy-dog.

"I'm thirty-three years old."

"So?" He moves up to my thigh.

"I don't have many more years to be cute."

"Was *he* cute?"

"Who?"

"Max."

"Boyish."

"That's what you are. Turn over."

I turn over. "What? Boyish?"

He begins on my feet again. "Yeah."

"But not your type."

"If I ever said I was hot for you," Joe says, making circular motions across the sole of my foot with his hand, "you'd shit in your pants. You like this—game."

"I want to be wanted," I say.

"Um." He massages my ankle. "Think of something else to want from me."

⚊

"We used to go everywhere together. We were very tight. Do you think I was trying to avoid men? Then she moved into the city. We used to go to concerts and Lincoln Center and to plays. She had all sorts of friends. Maybe they thought we were an item. You know? But she knew who I was. What I was. But I thought she could deal with it. *I* never brought it up. She went dancing with us a lot. She wasn't a fag hag but almost. She had lots of gay friends. But I was her closest friend. We used to talk all the time. On the phone every day, when I came in to see her, all the time. About everything. And music. We shared music in common, very much. Then one day she just says she can't see me anymore. I thought initially she had, you know, like a boyfriend finally. But I asked why and she said finally that I wasn't any good for her anymore. Just like that. And she hung up on me. That night she called me again and she'd taken all these pills. I drove in and took her to the hospital and she said once in the car, just once, 'It's your fault.' I didn't know what she meant. 'Were you in love with me?' I finally asked when I visited her at home after she got out. 'No,' she said. 'Go get a boyfriend. I'm tired of looking at your face.' And I didn't see her anymore. That's why I went into therapy. There are three things I want to cure. Her, not cumming, and my job."

"So you're doing 'not cumming' now."

"Yeah."

I sat across Joe's hips. His head was in his arms. I worked on his shoulders. The muscles were like India rubber.

"Music. What about music? You did music in school."

"That. I wasn't good enough. And you know? She ruined music for me. After that. I never listen to real music anymore. Just disco. I never listen to classical music."

"Why don't you try to, you know, get back into it?"

"Naw."

I put my fingers into his hair and massaged his scalp. He turned his head, face down, into the pillow.

"Feels good," he said, voice muffled.

"Joe? Maybe that's the key."

"What?"

"Music. Instead of Korvettes."

"That's number three."

"Maybe music—not doing it, not listening to it—maybe that's all three."

"I was very good at it once," he said, turning his profile to me again. (I dropped back down to his neck.) "I was very, very good. I won a scholarship. But I was not good enough."

"What's 'not good enough'?"

"You," he said, turning under me and sliding out, "you're prejudiced. *You* like me."

"So?"

"I don't exactly like myself."

A

A visit with my political friend in his Lower East Side railroad flat. I climb the stairs and walk down the dim hall, rap on the flimsy door. It stinks in the corridor. I often think, on these visits, that my political friend (whose father is a vice president with Kodak and who grew up in the Rochester suburbs) has chosen to live down here not merely due to the exigencies of the poverty his life's work has imposed on him, but for the strong odor of *nostalgie de la boue* that saturates this part of the world.

Hair all in a mess, clad in a shapeless T-shirt, jeans and tennis shoes, my political friend greets me at the door with a soul kiss and a revolutionary handshake rather too complicated for me ever to have mastered. Vivaldi is on the record player. A cluster of babies'-breath, a bit shopworn and dusty, sits in a ceramic jar (made for him by one of the kids at the daycare center where he works) in the center of the kitchen table. Above it, taped to the wall, is a reproduction of a piece of Socialist Realism depicting *workers militant* with pipe wrenches in their huge fists, hunky enough in their athletic postures to appeal to my decadent bourgeois tastes. . . .

His apartment is clearly the abode of a split personality rather provisionally integrated. But it has been this way since I met and tricked with him years ago. A variorum set of Marx sits cheek by jowl with dog-eared copies of *Hollywood Babylon* and *The Annotated Lolita*. A vintage *Easter Parade* poster (my friend once wrote a scholarly paper entitled "Judy Garland As Androgynous Ikon") leans up against a bookcase containing, among other works, books by Germaine Greer, Anaïs Nin, Shulamith Firestone, Kate Millet, and Ti-Grace Atkinson—his particular guides and muses. On a lower shelf lies a lone copy of *After Dark* magazine—"research."

In fact, if books *do* furnish a room, this shabby hole is furnished—with stacks, shelves and teetering towers of books, with pamphlets, back issues of obscure newsletters, journals, mimeographed study guides. There are also piles

of manila folders packed with news clippings, ancient man-
ifestoes, conference agendas, doctoral theses, dossiers. . . .

I'm sure there's a file on *me* in there somewhere.

Once, several years ago, when we were in the midst of
our brief, abortive affair, my political friend took me down
to City Hall. It was the day of one of the numerous defeats
the gay rights bill has suffered in the City Council. Immediately following the predictably negative vote, my
friend took me by the hand and dragged me onto the
approach to the Brooklyn Bridge, where he promptly sat us
down to block the rush-hour traffic. We were arrested. In
the paddy wagon, he turned to me and said, "Our love has
been sealed in blood," though neither of us was bleeding.

And I stuck with him—through conferences, meetings, long dreary afternoons marching, through the disso-
lution of our little affair, and beyond. We danced at the
Firehouse together in the first years of the Gay Activists
Alliance. Every Saturday night we danced at the Firehouse.
And though even my dancing friend will acknowledge that
dancing all began at the Firehouse, on that grubby SoHo
street, dancing inexorably moved elsewhere, into chic discos
and dance bars, onto the airwaves, into the suburbs. My
friend was left behind, standing in the ashes of the mysteri-
ously torched Firehouse, trying to salvage the files. And I
danced on, into precincts where those of us who danced
every Saturday night at the Firehouse would not have been
allowed. And into the arms of—Max. Max, as apolitical as
they come. Defected. I was tired of marching and arguing.
Tired of the war for my soul my political friend felt he had
been waging all those years. But not too tired to keep on
dancing. . . .

Not surprisingly, he is stuffing envelopes—for an anti-
nuclear power demonstration. (He is a prime mover in Fags
Against Nukes.) He bids me pull up a rickety folding chair
and help him.

"So how did you like the Island?" I ask.

"That," he says with a dismissive wave of the hand.

"That's not real." And he goes on to fill me in on the usual meetings and intramural squabbles and says he's picked up again on his consciousness-raising group (my actor friend once called it "the oldest floating crap game in New York"; but I wonder, if I'd *really* gotten involved, if I might be better off now; but I dismiss the thought) and tells me it isn't a CR group anymore for it has metamorphosed into another *study* group—Wilhelm Reich and Oscar Wilde.

"You really ought to drop by some Tuesday," he says. "We're into some fascinating stuff. Next week I'm reading a paper on 'Firbank As Anarchist.' "

Ronald Firbank? The novelist? *The* Firbank? Of the powdered rice paper and the scarlet fingernails?

"Haven't you ever read *Concerning the Eccentricities of Cardinal Pirelli*? A vicious attack on the Church. Mind-blowing."

I haven't, but my novelist friend tells me that Firbank's lifelong ambition, since he was rejected for the priesthood, was to be a member of the Papal Guard—even though he had neglected to provide himself with Swiss forebears. . . .

"Why don't you drop by?" he asks.

I fondly remember how, when I broke up with Max, my friend made an effort to introduce me to "nonthreatening" men. But of course *all* gay men—I hated them all at that point—even the nice ones with the ponytails.

"I'm . . .busy Tuesday nights," I say.

Of all my friends, my political friend is the last to learn about my sex therapy. Not that he is a prude. *He* goes to the *baths* for sex, on discount nights. But his opinion of therapy-in-general is as clear-cut as his opinions on all things: shrinks are, by definition, charlatans, out to exploit gays, women, children, the aged, all other minorities—in order to maintain heterosexual male supremacy.

"*Every* Tuesday? I thought your therapy group"—he lowers his voice to intone the awful words—"meets on Wednesdays. Or did you"—his face brightens—"drop out?"

"No. I'm just . . .busy."

"Doing what?"

Guilt gains the upper hand. What am I so afraid of?
"Uh, well, I'm not sure what you'll think about this. . . ." He
knows about my problem, but he *is* so opinionated.

"You know," I say, "I've been having this problem in
bed. . . ."

He sets down an envelope and covers my hand with his.
That heart of gold. That heart would embrace human-
kind. . . .

"I'm . . .doing sex therapy."

He cocks his head to one side, like someone who
believes he *might* have heard an explosion, but very far
away.

I briefly describe our progress so far. I try to keep it
objective.

During my recitation, my friend does not cease squeez-
ing my hand. My knuckles turn white. One of them actually
pops.

"You're hurting my fingers," I say in conclusion.

I disengage my hand. He turns back to his envelopes.

"Aren't you going to say anything?'

"You need help," he says, tight-lipped, stuffing his
fliers.

I pick up a stack of fliers and fold them.

"Yes," I say. "I need help."

"Have you ever thought that it might not be *you*?"

I set down the fliers.

"Me? Isn't it? I mean, really."

"That maybe it's the men?"

"Oh," I say, laughing a little laugh. I keep on folding.
"In my more paranoid moments."

"And so now," he says quietly, "you have to change your
sexuality to fit the world. Adapt. *That* has a familiar ring."

I set down the fliers.

"This so-called therapy," he says, not looking at me.
"Don't you know what it is? Behavioral modification."

"Yes. . . ."

"Pure Skinner, Danny. Exactly what they use to try to *change* us. Because *we* don't fit. And Virgil. . . ."

"Virgil's my therapist. Virgil's *gay*."

"What a fascist!"

I stand up and walk to the window. What I actually want to do is piss all over the fliers, all over him.

"A fascist?" I say, tone deadly.

"Maybe that was a little strong."

"Bullshit. That's what it was."

"Not letting you have sex with other people. It's pure deprivation brainwashing. In order to reprogram you to follow his commands."

I don't answer. Looking down into the little Jewish cemetery that abuts his building, I reflect that he has given a rather apt description of what I secretly fear Virgil *might* be doing to us.

"If only it were that easy," I say.

"I'm sorry I hurt your feelings."

"No you aren't," I say, wheeling on him. "I just wish you wouldn't drag politics into everything. Marx and Marcuse aren't going to help me with my problem. . . ."

"Marx actually has a lot to say about—"

"It doesn't have *anything* to do with politics. *None* of this has anything to do with politics. *Max* didn't have anything to do with politics. *You* didn't have anything to do with politics. . . ." (Oh, low blow, bringing up our pathetic affair.) "This is my own personal business."

I turn around to the window again. I can hear him slipping fliers into envelopes behind my back. After a while, he says, "The personal is the political."

"Oh, don't start mouthing slogans at me," I snap.

I sit down beside him and, furiously, stuff a few fliers.

"I'm glad you told me," he says after a while. "But if it's your own personal business, why bother to tell *me*?"

"Because you're my friend," I say softly.

"Who can't understand human misery," he says, his mouth a drawn line now.

"Of course that's not—"

"And Max *did* have to do with politics," he says. His face looks hurt.

"How's that?"

"All the time I knew him," my political friend says, inserting antinuke fliers into envelopes, "I never saw Max touch you in public."

It's true.

A

When Joe comes to see me the next night, the peck he gives me on the cheek (this pro-forma intimacy is allowed) is more perfunctory than usual.

"What's wrong with *you?*" I ask, opening up the goodies he's brought. (He insists on supplying us, in exchange for the apartment, even though he has to drive such a long way.)

He sits on the couch, staring down at the floor.

"I met someone," he says.

"Met someone? When?"

"Saturday night."

"Oh?" I stop unpacking the cookies, the juice, the fruit. I wonder if he's just dramatizing. He does that sometimes. "Who? What do you mean?"

"This real cute guy," he says darkly.

"And?" He is just that much younger than I. I can remember how it was at twenty-six. . . .

He looks up at me. I could swear his eyes are reddened, moist. "And nothing."

And I feel right then that it must be worse, to be in our predicament, at twenty-six, than it is for me now. . . .

"You know his name?"

"Yeah. He's a friend of my friend. Sure."

"Well, when this is over, you can get together with him, can't you?"

He sneers and looks back down at the rug. "If it's ever over."

I know what he means. It isn't just a matter of plumbing, this—disability. We've been kidding ourselves, pretending that it was, all these weeks. I've been withholding more than my cum. And I can't help myself. And neither can Joe.

Joe has never cum with another person in his life. He told me about the last time he had sex—saying the word with that wry turn of inflection identical to mine.

The boy (he couldn't have been more than nineteen) followed Joe around from bar to bar. Joe had no real interest in him, though he was attractive and friendly—and so hot. But the boy couldn't get enough of Joe and was so persistent that at 2:00 A.M. Joe agreed to go to the motel with him.

Joe sat down on the bed. The boy took off his clothes, sat down beside Joe, and began unbuttoning Joe's shirt. Joe was very hard, very excited. He wasn't drunk. He never drinks.

The boy lay on top of Joe. Joe hoped he would get it off quickly. He was so hot Joe knew he would cum right away, but if the boy found out *he* couldn't, it would be a drag. Better fast. Better now.

The boy urged Joe to finish undressing, and he did. They sucked each other. Kissed a bit. Sucked. Joe sucked the boy a long time. "Don't you want to cum?" he asked the boy.

"I'm waiting. I want to cum with you."

"That's all right," Joe said. "I'm a little tired tonight."
Eventually, under protest of sorts, the boy came.

They left the motel and said goodbye on the sidewalk outside, shaking hands rather formally.

Joe found his car and started it up. He thought about the boy, the boy's body. He was more frustrated than he'd been when he'd left home after showering, dressing (big deal, big night out at the bars, sure), and driving twenty miles to the bar. He was more frustrated than he'd ever been in his life, if that was possible.

He took out his cock, driving home in the dark. He jacked off, thinking about the boy and the boy's body.

That was the week before we met. Joe says he looked forward to meeting the nice older man, me, who was "more experienced" than he.

⚐

Even if my political friend doesn't attempt to hide his disapproval over what I'm doing, he does seem rather fascinated by it. Just now, on the phone, he asked me for detail after detail—nothing prurient, all quite academic. This surprised me, and I wondered if he needed help himself. Maybe he's started another file.

The rest of my friends seem to think it's all a little dizzy and—even my novelist friend, who felt it was such an adventure—more than a little unnecessary. They pretend to be interested, but hearing about my sex therapy bores them as much as hearing about therapy in general. Let's face it: baby-oil massage is hardly a conversation grabber. All of them, I know, must be secretly of the opinion that all I need is the love of a good man.

Otherwise I've kept the dirty secret (am I the only one? besides Joe?) just that. I'm reading this new novel in which a character says that men with small cocks are the lepers of the gay world; but I don't think that's really so much the case. Those who can't get it up, whatever the size of it, they are the true lepers. With us "slow comers" running a close second.

The "dysfunction" cuts two ways: the man you're in bed with views you with disdain and fear—disdain because he is fearful, knows it could be him.

Oh, the answers to my problem are so easy and evident. Fear of men. Fear of getting hurt. Fear of losing control. Fear of not performing. But I didn't know how complicated things could get. I have a new fear: fear—yes, this now—of succeeding.

⚑

Joe and I talk, talk, talk.

Not always about clothes.

Tonight he sat on my back, massaging my shoulders. He was hurting my back, but I was too "shy" to ask him to get off. So I suffered and was mad at him for being so inconsiderate. "Why didn't you just tell me?" he asked afterward. That seems to be the sixty-four-thousand-dollar question.

I'm intrigued by this "shyness" Joe and I both seem to have raised to a high art. Perhaps not cumming is, at base, an elaborate means of making sure we stay isolated. And, if so, shyness is a good weapon in the battle. And we are mad when people don't do the work of communicating for us.

"You absolutely must tell each other everything," Virgil says. "No matter how trivial or stupid, how embarrassing it might seem at the time. And things no lovers would tell each other. That's our only rule."

Nothing hidden. All out on the table, in plain view. Maybe this is the way we'll learn to trust each other, a trust that's growing slowly but very slowly. It will not make lovers per se out of us. What will it do?

We try.

⚑

Thoreau said something to the effect of, "If I knew a man were coming to my door with the express purpose of doing me good, I would not be at home." Joe must feel that way about my nagging. I give him lots of advice—get out of that house, make new friends, get a new job.

I told him at the beginning that I had this bossy side and that I would always preface these incursions with "Big Brother says." I have been. But I want to approach Joe as an equal, as the partner he is, not impose my experiences on him or do his work for him. The fact that he is very needy and lonely makes this difficult.

And I'm also fighting my desire to lecture and patronize Joe for another reason. To do so is to keep him at arm's length, to deny we are having a relationship. A most peculiar relationship, but a relationship all the same.

A

Joe is going to visit his sister in California this week, so no sex therapy. Really, I welcome the vacation and I know he's happy to be going away for a while.

Our discussions are getting pretty intense. With no real evidence to base it on, I feel we're somehow getting in deeper and deeper. Our therapy is like *No Exit*—we circle around the same problems (responsiveness, lack of, etc.) all the time. Massage is boring. Joe is often sullen and snappish, silent. I am impatient with his depression. How long will Virgil keep up massage? We already know a great deal about each other. We like each other. What more does Virgil want?

We've been having little spats. All very childish. Not like lovers at all.

My ass.

A

Fire Island again this weekend. Took the train out Saturday morning. Rained all afternoon, so we stayed inside playing Scrabble. The rain let up in the early evening, but by the time we were ready to go out dancing (at one) it started again. So my Fire Island friend pulled out some cheap plastic ponchos he keeps for such contingencies, and we went down to the Sandpiper in the rain.

We danced for an hour or so, then he announced he was "going out trashing." "In all this rain?" I exclaimed. And he left me with a couple of guys we'd been dancing with. I went home about three, hot and weary, nicely so. My dancing friend (the *wife* of one of the decorators had pushed him out this time) was snoring away in the Princess Suite. I went to bed in the other bedroom.

At dawn, my Fire Island friend slipped into bed beside me. Instinctively, I snuggled up to him. But he gently urged me over to my own side of the bed. . . .

Sitting on the beach and viewing the passing bodies with appreciation and detachment. Sunday. Utter serenity. The way one might view a fine Monet, or better yet, a Winslow Homer landscape/seascape. All that turbulence, so far away, viewed through this remote lens. . . .

"How was it?" my actor friend asked over the phone Sunday night.

"Heaven," I said. "It's the only way to go."

"Had a good time, huh?"

"I never realized how wonderful the Island could be. The secret, of course, is to abolish every single thought of sex from your mind. . . ."

"That's the most perverse statement I've ever heard," he said.

A

Back from his vacation, Joe called me at work today. "Are we still on for tonight?"

"Of course," I said. "How was California?"

"My sister's kids are *big*," he said. "Everyone kept asking me when I was going to get married."

"What'd you say?"

"Oh, Danny, you're going to hate me," he said.

"But why?"

"I told them I didn't know. That 'the right girl' hasn't come along."

"Why would I hate you for that?"

"I don't know. Well, the way *you* live. . . ." There was a silence on the other end of the line. I heard a cash register ring in the background.

"My parents don't ask me *anything* anymore," I said.

"But they *know* you're gay."

"Exactly."

"That's what *I* thought," he said. "I don't know if I'm ready for that."

Another pause.

"You want anything special tonight?" he asked. "How about brownies? You like brownies?"

"You want to give me more zits?" I joked. "Anything."

"Well, I'll bring us something."

"Just bring yourself," I said. "I missed you."

"Did you?"

"Sure."

Another pause, then we said goodbye.

⚐

The way I live. Thinking how it's a long way from the utility room in the dorm basement where I used to go late Saturday nights with this guy from down the hall who I never acknowledged in public, not even when we bumped up against each other at the mailboxes.

A long way from that interminable winter in Vermont, all alone dreaming of men, snow neck-high around the house.

A long way from the night in college when I tried to kill myself because my best friend got engaged and I was the only homosexual in the state of Illinois.

New York fags. How spoiled we are. For every one of us, with our dysfunctions, there are hundreds of kids Out There longing to change places with us; longing behind screen doors in one-horse towns; longing, without understanding the longing, for their English professors; longing and loitering around the Greyhound Bus Terminal.

For every one of me, there's a Joe—in the loving bosom of his family.

Thinking about my family, far away, who ask nothing of, nothing from me any longer.

Should Joe move to New York? San Francisco? Atlanta? Is it really necessary? What does he have to become? Who?

⚠

"What are we?" Hands working around his groin.

"You want my opinion?" Head tilted back on the pillow, eyes closed.

"You brought it up."

"Will you write down what I say?"

"What do you mean?" Stroking his belly.

"If I say what I think? In your journal?"

I stop. "I don't write everything down."

"Sure you do. That's what you do. You write in that journal."

"Not everything."

"Don't stop."

I go back to his belly.

"Why not?" He is looking at me now, curious.

"Too lazy."

"But you do lots."

"Um-hm." Fine skin, smooth, tan. He's been doing exercises, working out.

"Well, you can write this down: we're buddies."

"Buddies."

"Yeah. Working on being fuck buddies."

"I thought we were 'sisters.' "

"Naw. Not anymore. Will you write down my opinion?"

"Sure."

"Just want you to put down *my* side."

I put my palms on his chest, rub with circular motions, outward.
He sighs.
"Feel good?"
"Yeah." Then, "I don't like that word 'sisters.' "

⚑

Joe and I sit naked on the floor, porno magazines spread out around us. We have each been through these magazines before and know the models intimately. We have favorites, of course. Different types. Joe, the Italian-American, likes the All-American Football Jock, preferably hairless. I, the WASP, like the diminutive, dark-eyed Latins, lightly muscled but mature, preferably hairy. He is too tall for my taste. I am too short, not hunky enough for his. But every once in a while we surprise each other. This is the first time we have "compared" together, not an assignment but a friendly inspiration, to share our fantasies. At first unsure of our roles, we are now (we have compromised) sister/buddies.
"What about him?"
"Naw. Him."
"*Chacun à son goût.*"
"What?"
"Nothing."

⚑

I furtively consign my speculations to these pages. There's no place for them between the two of us.

⚑

"I thought you were getting sexy there," I said to Joe the other night, explaining why at one point I got so hard so fast.
"I wasn't." Rather piqued that I'd again impugned his

integrity. "It's like tickling," he said. "If you want to be tickled, you will be. I wasn't getting sexy."

He's waiting for the order to get sexy. Can he help it if he *is* sexy sometimes without wanting to be?

We are two healthy (if dizzy) young men, naked together most of the time, hands all over each other. There is sex here; you can bet on it. But he doesn't like to deal with the fact.

Perversely (or out of boredom) I sometimes let my fingers stray into the crack between those gorgeous buns and, instead of using the side of my hand, probe at the puckered asshole, and wonder what he might be thinking— but I stop myself, of course, from reaching down between his legs, under him, and running my hand up along the underside of his cock. I tell him afterward. Always. I stop when I remember that it is Joe whose body lies under my hands, whose dark rich flesh sometimes twitches a bit under my fingers, like the flank of a horse shuddering in its sleep.

For Joe is sleeping—not literally but sexually. I fear to wake him up before his time and I'm elated by my evident power to do so—for a moment—until I remember he is Joe, my partner, my sister, my buddy. And that this is not (as my political friend divined) entirely under our control.

It is Virgil who says when.

A

"Danny's too polite."

"What do you mean?" Virgil asked.

"He's polite, but we're very different people."

Virgil considered that for a while. "I don't think Danny's a snob," he said, rather squirming (I thought) under his shrink's reluctance to express an opinion, *any* opinion.

"He's not a snob," Joe said. "But I don't know what he wants out of me." He was stroking the arms of the chair, a clear sign that he was angry—I've learned to tell.

Joe looked away and studied the curtain billowing in the breeze from the street. There was a long silence that

went unbroken by Virgil or me. Joe was trying to pretend
that what he'd brought up had been resolved.
"We're friends," I said. I was hurt by what he'd said.
He looked at Virgil and asked, "Do we have to be?"

▲

We are different people, and he is right, we're coming
up against the boundaries of our differences. But there is a
language we're learning. I know Joe through his body better than through anything he says. The body is taking over,
and any other language is beginning to ring false—as we
chat about movies and clothes and disco and what we are to
each other.
"The mind remembers," a famous flamenco dancer
once said, explaining why she practiced ten hours a day,
"but the body forgets." Joe expresses no admiration, no
affinity, no lust for my body, but slowly he is teaching my
body—which has forgotten the touch of anyone else—how
to feel again.

▲

After Joe left tonight, I flashed on Max. Don't think of
him much lately. But in my mind's eye he is standing there
with his hand on the doorknob, talking. At least his mouth is
moving. I'm fixated on the fact that he has his hand on the
doorknob, as if, like 007, he must be ready to make a quick
escape. Throughout our entire relationship he was on the
verge of taking a powder. At least that was the threat,
ubiquitous, omnivorous. He warned me at the beginning
that he wouldn't fight, that he would walk out if we fought,
that he had no stomach for fighting. So we didn't fight. And
he couldn't leave. So he dematerialized.
He used to say I was the love of his life. What do you do
with someone who lies in bed with you saying you're the love
of his life but refuses to have sex with you?
We were just talking, so why was his hand on the door-

knob? Ah, yes. We were talking about money. Fifty-fifty. As in love, so in parting. I was grief-stricken. He was relieved. And, oh yes. The barked knuckles, dressed and bandaged, that lay in my lap.

"You should have hit *him*," said my novelist friend, "not my wall."

A

Poor Max. His lover went crazy. When he was in L.A. that last time, I had a nervous breakdown. Perhaps not so incidentally, but I had it.

Max had written me, two weeks before, the first letter, the first contact in weeks, that Halloween he went Hollywood. That Halloween he went dancing at Studio One. He went dancing at Studio One with Sandy Duncan. The next day he wrote:

The costumes were a riot and we danced and laughed. It is the first time I've had a chance to blow off steam. All the lights and music and general insanity caused all of us to feel good. I let out many days of built-up anxiety. I ended up with someone. It was wonderful because it was a stranger. We had pure sex for sex sake—no obligation, no talk of business—just escape. The only time in ages I haven't felt guilt or obligation or pressure. It has been a long time since I had sex without love. I really felt free.

We'd planned for me to meet him there, but he asked me not to come. "We really wouldn't have any time together. It would be bad for us."

He hadn't written me for weeks or answered my phone calls. "We are in a crisis," he added, unnecessarily. "Again. How I wish our life could be carefree."

Poor Max. Did he know his letter made sure it was already over before he finally did come home?

❂

There was a large star-burst cut into the finish on the floor in the little alcove off the living room. A big red Deco table sat in that alcove, and on it a large frosted glass globe a friend had given me years before. Above the globe hung an Erté print, a perfect match for the table, the first of Max's purchases with his new money.

Newly arrived home, Max walked back and forth over the scars on the floor, the floor we'd refinished together, in pre-money times. But he didn't notice the scars. Finally he did ask what had happened to the globe.

"I broke it," I said neutrally.

"Oh," he said, and walked back into the study.

I didn't tell him what else I'd broken the night I received his letter. I hadn't broken anything of his.

❂

I found myself face down on the kitchen floor, unable to move.

"This is something new," I remember thinking. My mind was bobbing, disembodied, on a vast inky-black lake. "This is something new." My face felt as if it were smirking.

I managed to wiggle my fingers. "Still there." I was out of breath. I'd fallen with a big Whump. "What am I doing here?" My ribs hurt. "I have things to do."

I'd been doing so many things. I'd been accomplishing things. The bathroom was very clean. The bed had fresh sheets on it. The plants were fed and watered. All my clothes were laundered and pressed. The refrigerator contained my favorite foods. The bills were paid. I was caught up at work.

Like a person preparing for suicide. Exactly.

But that was ridiculous. I had no intention of committing suicide.

I looked at a chair leg looming large in my field of vision. . . . A corner of the stove. . . . The baseboard. . . . A long dribble of paint off the baseboard had pooled and dried on the linoleum next to the stove. "Never noticed *that* before." Must get up and find a razor blade, scrape up the paint. I closed my eyes. A black tide advanced, crested—the waves in a movie studio tank—with blue-black caps. I opened my eyes just in time.

My canvas bag lay next to me, on top of my jacket. The day's mail fanned out across the floor like playing cards.

I thought of poor Max, so far away. He would blame himself for this. "Satisfied?" I said to myself. "Got yourself good and fucked up? That'll show him, huh?" But it was not Max, of course. This was something new.

I swallowed. A mistake, for when you swallow you close your eyes, just for a second, even—spreading ink. A sudden cinch in my belly, as if someone had taken a fold of flesh, twisted hard.

The phone bill, unpaid, was lying almost directly under my nose.

"Can't just lie here. Have to get up eventually."

Then I was lying on my back. It had taken no force of will, no extraordinary effort. But I didn't remember turning over. The light fixture in the middle of the ceiling swayed—the approaching shock waves in the movie *San Francisco*, remember the shot?—and I clamped my teeth shut.

"Now you're seeing things with your eyes open."

I thought of poor Max, so far away, so busy. Dare I call Max?

A

"Then I thought," I said to Virgil, my new shrink—I was unable to meet his eyes, the academic expression on this stranger's face—"that you might have a nervous breakdown and still be able to know you're having one."

"Yes," he said.

"And that I was about to have one."

"_____"

I gripped the arms of the chair. Nausea again, as if I were a piece of cargo swinging out on a line, from one great ship to another, over that black sea.

"How did I get this way?"

"That's what we'll have to find out."

⚠

I got up off the kitchen floor and dialed a few numbers. Finally I reached my feminist friend.

"Something's happening," I said, feeling quite calm. It was the voice of someone who looks up from the pavement and sees a man jumping from a window ledge, high above.

⚠

"How do you feel today?"

"Shaky. I didn't go to work. I slept all day. I tried to call Max, my lover."

"_____"

"He wasn't in. And he hasn't called back. My friend called him last night. He left a message on her machine. He said he'd call back. He hasn't called back."

"Close your eyes a minute, Danny. What do you feel?"

"Nothing."

"Okay."

"It isn't his fault I'm this way."

"_____"

"I have to help myself."

"_____"

"But why won't he call?"

⚠

The vodka blazed up in my stomach.

"You're shaking all over," my friend said. "Maybe you should put on a sweater."

"No." I held her hand tight.

"Shall I call Max?"
"It isn't Max," I said.
"What is it? Who said it was Max?"
"It's me. There's Max, but there's no me left."

▲

"I gave it all to Max."
"How gave it to Max?" Virgil asked.
"And he didn't even ask me for it."

▲

Max came home a few weeks later. I asked him to come see Virgil with me. I had a lot of problems of my own I had to help myself with, but maybe we could talk to Virgil about us.
"If you think it would help you," he said.
I turned away.

▲

"You have to stop crying," my novelist friend said. He slathered iodine over my barked knuckles and held my hands down on the sheets to let it dry. "You have to stop crying," he said. "You're only making yourself sick. I'm going to go back to bed now and you're going to stop crying. You should have hit *him*, not my wall."
Poor Max locked himself in the bedroom. His lover was so crazy.

▲

"You've been living in a fantasy," Virgil finally said. "Your lover doesn't want to live with you. He doesn't want to share his life with you. He wants you to let him go."
"But why?" I wept.
"Ask him."

But Max wasn't saying. "I can only think of work," he said. I knew he was telling the truth.

⚐

I moved on a Saturday in December. Friday night Max came into the living room, where all my boxes were piled.

"What do you want me to do?" he asked. For two years he had been asking me that.

"Nothing," I said. "Just let me out of here."

There wasn't one shred of reality about that moving day—except the envelope Max urged into my hand as I stood in the kitchen packing pots and pans into a barrel.

In the envelope was a check for the furniture, the paint, the shiny new floors, the blinds we'd put up at the windows, the hardware we'd replaced on the cabinets, the shower curtain and the new towels we'd bought for the bathroom, the hooks and eyes and nails and picture wire, the set of glass dinner plates, every rash or calculated purchase we'd made together. All fifty-fifty.

There was the check and there was a final note. He was sorry. I was still the love of his life—"so far."

⚐

"Whatever you do, don't start another hope chest," said my actor friend, unpacking the few plates I still had left after the Night of the Letter. "God. It's pure Dory Previn, isn't it?"

"Perhaps modern relationships," said my novelist friend, dropping a bunch of carnations into a mason jar and setting it on a stack of boxes in the center of my new room, "perhaps relationships should be counted like cats' and dogs' lives. In feline terms, then, Max and you lasted eighteen years!"

"What are you going to do now?" asked my feminist friend, meaning where was I going to start, which box.

But I thought she meant something else. "I don't know," I said, searching in a crumpled paper bag for my medication. "Try to figure out how all this happened."

▲

"What was he like?"
"He was the best roommate anyone could have."
"Come on."
"He was very quiet. Nice. Well-liked. Everyone liked him. My friends liked him."
"How'd you meet him?"
"In a bar. Where else?"

▲

It was the Wildwood, on the Upper West Side. That next summer we ran into each other there again. We hadn't seen each other since I left.

"Your hair's longer," I said.

He turned around. "Yours is shorter," he said.

We talked a bit. He'd been to Europe. A film deal hadn't panned out, but there was something new on a back burner.

I wasn't in love with him anymore. But nothing else had changed really. Not in the way we behaved toward one another. I could either have made love to him or strangled him. Perhaps both. He knew it, too.

He didn't ask me any questions about myself.

I wanted to tell him how well things were going for me. I wanted to prove to him that I wasn't crazy. Mainly I wanted to get through this chance encounter just to be able to say I had.

We filled each other in on what our friends were doing. When there was nothing more to say, I left the bar and went home. I was trembling, but it wasn't because of Max, the Max I'd just left in the Wildwood.

There was a new Max, inside me, that the real Max no longer resembled at all. It was, of course, a Max more real than the stranger I'd just seen.

▲

"How'd you meet him?"
"In a bar. Where else?"
"Yeah?"
"But we had friends in common. He had great credentials."
"You moved in together."
"Nine months after we met. It was a long courtship by prevailing standards."
"That was a joke, right?"
"Right."
"What happened?"
"Oh, we played house for a while. But it became obvious fairly early on that he didn't really want to live with anyone. He *thought* he did."
"So what'd you do?"
"Held on. Made it worse. 'You're always watching me,' he said once. He was right."
"I know what he meant," Joe says, holding my oiled foot in his hand.
"He never looked at me," I say, after Joe has gone back to kneading the foot. "Just like you."
"*I* look at you."
"Not as much as I *watch* you."

▲

Am I the only one? Who waited so long and wanted so much that nothing else would do?

With all the ritual concentration of bullfighters suiting up for the ring, Joe and I prepare for our first night of "sex."

As usual we are going to massage. But we have also selected and set close at hand our porno—pictures for Joe, stories for me. When we finish massaging, we are to begin to jack each other off. Then, when we get hot, we're to finish the job with our porno in separate rooms.

The theory, as Virgil's outlined it for us (and as we've read in *The Joy of Gay Sex* half a dozen times by now), is to approach each other gradually over a series of sessions—from the other room, from across the room, with our backs to each other, then side by side—and eventually we will arrive at mutual (if not simultaneous) orgasm.

We are giggly and self-conscious. I can't look Joe in the eye. I get hard while he's massaging me, even before he touches my cock—just like the old days.

Finished massaging, we take a little break for iced tea and cookies. The atmosphere in the room is heavily charged with anticipation, with contained hilarity. It is as if two Camp Fire Girls had just been asked to appear in a movie called *Vampire Pussies on Parade*.

We lie down side by side. I take Joe's cock in my hand. He grabs mine.

This is not massage. This is the real thing.

If so, why do I feel as if I'm right back in the basement spare room with my cousin Glen at twelve ("I'll show you mine. . . .") and scared that my parents will come bursting into the room with a search warrant and pistols at the ready?

I'm very hard. Joe takes a little longer. As he pumps away at me, I feel . . . if he . . . does it just a bit longer. . . .

The idea that I might cum then and there is terrifying. I ask Joe to stop for a while. I felt that I *could* have cum, but I have thrashed around on that particular plateau many times before. Was it an illusion this time as well?

Joe's eyebrows rise on his tanned forehead. He is thinking, I find out later, that I am less fucked up than he. He must struggle for a moment to remember that not cumming is my problem, too. He feels faintly betrayed, a sinking disappointment. Will I pass him up? What kind of game have I been playing all these weeks? He falls back on the quilt and closes his eyes.

We begin again. When we can stand it no longer, we separate. I go into the bathroom, Joe stays where he is. I close the flimsy door, cursing my studio apartment. Put down the toilet seat and sit. Open my magazine. *Playguy* (Vol. 1, No. 5). Turn to "Pit Stop," one of my favorites.

I often use porno when I jack off, almost always recently. Joe seldom does, but is taking no chances tonight. I can hear the *Man's Image Calendar* (1977) pages rustling in the other room as Joe searches out his companion.

The shower next door comes on and I can hear voices. The toilet seat is cold and hard. I am semisoft.

HE IS STAKED OUT SPREAD-EAGLE IN THE GREASE PIT TO ROAST UNDER THE HOT TEXAS SUN

Next door, a woman's voice: "I could just go down there tomorrow and tell them. . . ."

THE YOUNGER GARAGE ATTENDANT TAKES OUT HIS COCK AND PISSES A LONG HOT STREAM INTO THE PIT, OVER HIS FACE AND CHEST. HE DOESN'T WANT TO, BUT HIS RAGING THIRST DRIVES HIM

TO OPEN HIS MOUTH, TO LAP UP THE GOLDEN LIQUID

From the other room, a moan. My foot jerks and taps against the bottom of the door.

"...And if they won't, then I'll just..." says the voice next door.

TRUSSED UP, BENT DOUBLE OVER THE BELT, THE GREASE GUN UNCEREMONIOUSLY THRUST UP HIS ASSHOLE

"You done, Danny?" Joe.

Jesus H. Christ! He's finished! I just about came in the living room with him and now I'm not going to cum at all. ...

RIDING BACK AND FORTH ON THE BIG ONE'S COCK

On the fucking toilet seat. ...

"UMF," HE PROTESTS, AS THE KID'S COCK SWELLS IN HIS MOUTH, STIFLING HIS CRIES

Cumming. ... Cumming. ...

What the fuck is Joe doing? Making coffee? He's making coffee!

Tight. ...

So ironic. I was so hot in there. ...

"LET ME HAVE A TURN," THE KID SAYS

Cumming. ...

PULLS OUT WITH A SLURP

Ah. ... Ah. ... Ah. ...

I cum.

"Joe?"

"Yeah?"

"You done?"

"Yeah. Want some coffee?"

⚓

Any resemblance between what Joe and I are doing now and "real sex" is purely coincidental.

Maybe that's good. The idea is to move—very gradually—from a nonthreatening situation (and what could be less threatening than the two of us sitting with our backs to each other, working away at ourselves like maniacs?) into a situation that would have frightened us before.

How much anxiety and fear have been wrapped up in my idea of "real sex"? That night with my cousin Glen, for instance, the first fabulous experience, tainted only (heightened?) by the fear of discovery. Over the years I've all but brought the F.B.I., the New York State Legislature, the Supreme Court—to say nothing of my parents—brought them all into the many rooms where I've had sex. (Let's try to forget for the sake of psychological clarity that they're there in the name of the law anyway.) And along the line I invented a new Board of Review as well: the International Faggots League for Purity in Sexual Performance. All of them stand at the foot of the bed, taking notes and commenting on my performance.

"Does he pleasure his partner?" (D+)

"Does he pleasure himself?" (F)

Etc.

But who could be deemed more innocent, more conscientious, more downright prepubescent than Joe and I? Who have not yet even looked each other in the eye during "the act"?

After body massage ("algebra" on Joe's scale of accomplishment) we *do* indulge in something that might be termed "foreplay." But then, of course, we separate.

⚐

Tonight we sat back to back. Our backs did not touch.

⚐

Tonight we lay side by side. We did not peek.

⚐

Tonight's the night.

A

"Too fast."

"Like that?"

"Yeah," I said. "Harder."

"Show me how you do it?"

I started jacking myself off.

"It says in the book you aren't supposed to look at it," Joe pointed out.

(So he'd been reading *The Joy of Gay Sex* again, where it says slow cummers keep themselves under an intense and debilitating scrutiny. . . .)

He took my cock in his hand again and tried to duplicate my manipulations. "That feels good," I said. (Off and on.)

"You want me to do you for a while?" I asked.

"Sure." He lay back and picked up a leaf of the now-dismantled calendar.

I jacked him a while.

"Do you have to look at that?"

"Yeah," he said. "Why not?"

"Are we supposed to?"

"Yeah," he said.

But I thought we were going to jack each other off tonight, that we at last had reached "real sex." And now he had his porno in his mitt.

"I thought we were going to . . . do each other," I said.

"We are. But we can use our porno, can't we?"

"I don't think so."

"Well, I'm going to use it," he said.

I lay back. We pumped each other's dick for a while, but it was clear there was a philosophical conflict here. He might have been lying beside me, but he was determined to put as much space between us as possible by sticking his nose into those damned pictures.

I released him and picked up my *Drummer* (Vol. 3, No. 22).

"Aren't you going to do me?" he asked.

"Not if you're using your porno," I said.

"I can use my porno."

"What's the point?" I said.

He glared at me a while, then sat up with his back half-turned to me.

I opened my *Drummer* and started reading "The Corporal in Charge of Taking Care of Captain O'Malley."

A MARINE BARRACKS LATE AT NIGHT. CAPTAIN O'MALLEY ENTERS WITHOUT WARNING, CATCHING THE CORPORAL OFF-GUARD (so to speak), COCK IN HAND

I jacked myself off. I came. ("All over the place," Joe commented dispassionately; Joe cums in white blobs, three or four of them, doesn't squirt like me.)

Joe was concentrating on Mr. April—bulging biceps, jockey shorts with a nickel-sized splotch on them, hard hat on his head for the sake of this one photo session. In reality he's anything *but* a hard hat: an amiable bodybuilder. . . .

Joe jacked himself off, remembering that "this is not a race," trying to picture that green glade to "relax." He couldn't, but finally he came.

"What was your fantasy?" I asked, even though he was still angry at me, and I know he hates to share them.

"I don't know." He wiped off his stomach with a towel. "I just thought of him . . .undressing." He turned over to throw the towel onto the floor, mumbled something.

"What?"

"In front of a bunch of women," he said, low.

"Oh."

A

"You can use whips, chains, cock rings, dildos, rubbers, whatever you like," says Virgil. "You're just determined to invent new Rules, aren't you?" he says to me.

"Yeah. I guess so."

"Do what you know you *can* do," he says to Joe. "Whatever's comfortable."

So I guess it was the best idea after all, to jack ourselves off after I'd put my foot into our first night of "sex."

⚠

These past few weeks, we've tried to jack each other off and failed time after time.

Forget the fact that Joe has cum in the presence of, aided and abetted by, another human being, for the first time in his life. He wants more. More!

He calls our therapy his "avocation." He no longer wants to go to the bars. "What for?" He misses his friends. He looks hassled, tired, and depressed. His narrow life, without the bars, without Friday and Saturday nights, is pressing in on him as never before.

Secretly I agree with him: this is taking too long. But I big-brother him (and the anger darts around in his dark eyes) that we have all the time in the world—that, as Virgil says, "Remember the tortoise and the hare" and "Too fast is slow in the end." Worrying, I say like a prissy Boy Scout, will guarantee our failure. In any case, we have not failed, I remind him, merely suffered a setback because we thought we'd finally get side by side and be able simply to jerk each other off and that would be that. . . .

"Do what you know you *can* do."

⚠

"But having someone jack me off is the hardest thing I know!" says my actor friend. "No one does it like I do it to myself."

⚠

It's clear to me now that what we're engaged in is nothing less than a complete restructuring of our sexual responses and a re-evaluation of all the suppositions and mythologies that have accompanied them in the past. We are formulating new principles to replace old, rigid Rules we carried into sex before this. To what extent everyone operates from those Rules (an unwritten, self-policing code of sexual etiquette), I don't know. Joe and I aren't typical, of course. But we feel there *is* something typical, some kind of behavior we can't live up to or fulfill. We can't be so atypical in that.

▲

Thinking how elementary are some of the lessons we've learned and how, like all issues in therapy, one has to arrive at them on one's own. Learning to say no, for instance, which comes so hard for us. Learning to say, or indicate, what we want. And learning *what* we want.

▲

Thinking about my coming-out. The first bar I ever walked into. Willy's on the Upper West Side. A music shop there now, at that time a black dance bar. The exultation I felt when I walked into Willy's that first night. As far as I knew, it was the only bar in New York. I stopped being the only homosexual in New York that night.

Friendly crowd, steaming atmosphere in that small room, tiny dance floor. I kept going back again and again. My first man in New York was an ex-Air Force sergeant. Saw him a few times, and one night as we were lying in bed he told me what a "dinge queen" was. It was assumed, he said, I was one. A white boy looking for a black Superman. And that's why some people weren't friendly.

"I want to keep seeing you," he said, "for myself. But you should find your own type, you know."

With great trepidation, I bought a bar guide at a local newsstand. Went downtown. And eventually I found a bar buddy, my teacher friend, and we made the rounds together in the Village. And I never went back to Willy's.

▲

Thinking about (can't help it) where I went wrong in my attitude toward men, the men I picked, the habits I acquired.

Thinking how this—this therapy—is perhaps a second coming-out. Or is it just growing up?

⚠

Using "Last Day on the Track" (*Numbers*, May 1978)— three-way with the Coach in the showers—I cum. I curl up next to Joe. He asks me not to. He doesn't know why. Just don't.

He never wants me to touch him, look at him.

⚠

In great despair about our failure.

Finally, tonight, when I couldn't bear to talk any longer, I got up off the couch, knelt next to Joe, and put my arms around him. I told him everything would be all right.

⚠

Something much more enormous than whether or not we can succeed at this is occurring between us. This something overshadows our dreary "exercises." The past few weeks of frustration have unveiled it, this something cold, alienating, and depressing about ourselves. We are not the "buddies" we hoped to be.

Joe is beyond my reach, especially when I hold his cock in my hand. I still avoid his eyes. Our fantasies (poor, tattered, exhausted fantasies) remain largely private, as remote as we are from each other, stale in the retelling.

Is it knowing we can only help each other so much? Is it that the new recognition of ourselves, reflected off the other, is too hard to take?

There is love between us, but that love has made us suffer in solitude, for it's inadequate to bring us together over the barriers of failure, the hopelessness we feel. We try to draw from our porno what the other can't supply.

Getting harder for me to bring myself off. The porno loses its power to take me away from Joe, and there is nothing in Joe for me to replace it with. Stalemated, I become trapped in my mind, can't stop thinking, fumble around, looking for a way out.

The other night I glanced over at Joe, above my magazine, and he was looking at me. He gave me a look of such pure intelligence that I flinched from it. His look said, "It's hopeless, isn't it? We're both alone in this."

Virgil tries to point out each particular incidence of negative thinking, how each ties into our old habits, how we are doing this to ourselves out of fear. Not that he talks this way, shrink that he is; I've deduced his method. Another defense? Another way to avoid success?

How do regular people have sex? Laughably, I've been asking myself that lately. For at this point I don't have any idea. Is the connection between people what's called love? And if not, isn't love just another elusive fantasy like those in my magazines? One of the many fantasies caught on the wing by people more forthright and aggressive than we are able to be?

⚠

"Obviously, he's trying to break you down," says my political friend of Virgil. "He's trying to render you so powerless that you'll be receptive to his instructions."

"But he doesn't give instructions. Not that way."

"I don't know what to say. Since it worked to a certain extent already."

"Thanks."

"For what?"

"Nothing. Where do you want me to put these posters?"

"Up and down Seventy-second Street, on every free surface you can find."

▲

To G.G.'s Barnum Room last night with my dancing friend. A middle-of-the-road disco on Forty-fifth Street once mainly frequented by drag queens and hustlers. A small room and bar off the main room. Stage and runway for drag shows. Trendy straights (it hit the media a few weeks ago), the Latin crowd, suburban gays, twosomes, threesomes, Punk Rock kids looking for something to bash their brains out on. The big room is two stories tall, surrounded on three sides by a balcony. At railing level, a net. Above that, trapezes and bars.

We buy our drinks, and I follow my friend (who has sprinted up the stairs ahead of me) to sit "ringside." Three boys and a girl (can one be sure?), all in gold lamé G-strings trimmed with black fur, swing from the bars or go-go on the narrow ledge over light panels that rise up from the floor below. A huge mirror ball in the middle of the ceiling turns slowly above the sequined and strobed discomaniacs below.

We sip our drinks, revving up to dance, taking in the place. "It was so fabulous the first time I came," my dancing friend says, "I was sure it would be a downer the second time around, but isn't it fabulous?"

A group of transvestites, very stylishly dressed, sits on one side of us. On the other, two boys with dark mustaches and wearing lumberjack drag. We indulge in some reprehensible speculations on where the acrobats on the swings come from and what they want out of life.

"Escaped from an Alabama trailer park."

"Marriage with an accountant."

Real slumming stuff.

Then, in darkness, one team replaces another. When the lights pulse up, we see an S&M tableau. Two boys stand over a girl, one pretending to beat her with a studded "belt" (a black satin sash set with silver beads), the other pretending to fuck her face. The shapes of the boys' breasts under their satin vests indicate they are in the midst of sex changes.

Buttocks convulsing in time with the music, sweat running down their backs and chests, the boys mime fucking the girl from every angle, in every conceivable position. But their studded crotches, violently thrusting, bumping, never touch her thighs or face. For the benefit of us here on the balcony, she opens her mouth and lets her red tongue flop out onto her chin, rolls the tongue around, rolls her eyes, makes faces that parody orgasm and insatiability as lewdly and coldly as those on satyrs in Roman frescoes.

Onto the trapezes. I watch an ass gyrating and pumping not five feet away from me, so close I can see the hairs gleaming wetly along the crack, the root of the balls between the legs. The spine is a deep indentation like a finger rut in soft clay. The muscles of the upper back fan out hard and well-defined, like the roots of the angels' wings poets place on beautiful boys' shoulder blades. . . .

My dancing friend turns to me and smiles. Am I enjoying myself? I nod. He turns back to the acrobats. The music screams, "Do or Die!" I have no desire to fuck this boy or anyone else.

 A

Yes, I love Joe. And I believe Joe loves me. But he's not infatuated with me, suffers no illusions about me, dislikes me a great deal as well, pities me to an extent that romance is out of the question. Our love exists in each of us like a hard kernel, a seed like those buried away in arid tombs, still capable of being germinated after thousands of years, but buried away in obscurity nevertheless. Our love for each other is an abstraction, an idea whose time will never come. Our caring for each other is substantial, empathetic. But our love for each other grows weekly more vestigial as we struggle not to fail ourselves and each other in this thing that neither of us quite understands. We are, after all, in this loverlike position only in order to seek out our own lovers freely. If our love achieves its purpose, it will no longer be needed.

I know now that however far we go together, Joe and I

will never kiss each other on the lips. Between us there will never be either that passion of the movie screens or that passion of the grope and spit-swap in the dark doorway.

My Fire Island friend half worries: "Will it transfer over to other people if you make it?" Then laughs. But he is serious. "Or will you be stuck with each other?"

I can't tell. This experience is devouring the past and the future, somewhat like some smaller cell takes in and incorporates a larger one.

⚠

Tonight Joe was lying on his back, flipping through a magazine, and I was sitting up, reading mine and jacking him off—just a quiet evening at home with the folks— taking it easy and waiting for him to wrap his hand around mine and guide it (Virgil calls this the "passive hand" technique), when I saw his legs stiffen and felt his cock throb, and he came.

He came.

He put his magazine down and we exchanged brief, disbelieving and rather fearful looks. Then we both smiled.

"Where did *that* come from?" I asked.

"I don't know," he said, wiping himself off. "It just happened."

Was it total relaxation or total boredom? How do we do it again?

Then, when we showered together and Joe was rinsing, I touched him on the side with my index finger, to point out that he'd missed a glob of lather. He flinched.

Later he told me he'd flinched in the shower because I was standing behind him and he was fantasizing that I was going to kill him—knife him, like *Psycho* or something. When I touched him, his heart stopped.

"Why?"

"Maybe I thought you were jealous," he speculated.

I was upset. I didn't know what kinds of vibes I might have been throwing off, though I knew I was happy for him.

"I must be jealous," I said. "I don't feel it very strongly, but I must be."

A

I'm lying on my back with my head propped up on the pillows, reading this story ("Studs and Suds Go Down at the Garage," *Numbers*, November 1978) about this mechanic and his young friend, who have lured this bodybuilder into the garage and he has pulled down his trousers ("hot in here") to reveal a pair of black bikini briefs packed tight with meat and after one blowjob sprawled out on the hood of a car he is ready to cum again so the boy goes down on him, then the bodybuilder pushes the boy's head away and stands him up and shucks his pants down and the boy sits on the bodybuilder's cock and the mechanic (getting a sudden inspiration) dips a broom handle in motor oil and shoves it up the bodybuilder's asshole and I am about to cum. . . .

I mean to ask Joe to take my prick in his hand and bring me off (if I can get him there in time; haven't been able to yet; or his hand has turned me off), but the only name I can think of is . . .

Max.

I drop back. I begin again. The mechanic is sticking an inquiring finger into the bodybuilder's asshole, the white buns squirm and squeak on the car hood, the boy rides the monster cock, the broomstick is pushed into the hole. . . .

Who is he? Joe. Right.

"Joe?"

His hand grasps my cock, and I am cumming.

A

"Simple," Virgil says. "You've been saving your cum for Max."

My dybbuk.

What a night! I finished massaging Joe and then he sat beside me and (very loverlike) ran his hands over my chest, cock, and balls, in circles around my cock, an abstracted look on his face, watching what my body was doing, doing the things I like.

I closed my eyes and immediately a fantasy popped into my head as I remembered "Father Figure" (*Playguy*, Vol. 1, No. 10), where this guy comes home from the navy and (Mom comfortably out of the picture) makes it in the kitchen with the Old Man ("He was looking at my pecs straining through my T-shirt..."). Then, alarmingly, *my own father* was in the picture, sitting at the kitchen table, feeling me up under the table. Whoa!

Joe was doing delicious things to my cock; we'd worked on that the other night.

In the kitchen in Nebraska.... I conjured up my Uncle Bob, the sailor, but my father wouldn't go away, his fingers fumbling for my fly, taking out my cock under the table, pretending to stir his coffee. I was rock hard. *Go with it,* I thought, and gave an involuntary little snort.

Joe's steady-unsteady rhythm didn't falter.

*Outside the window, leafy green trees. Sounds of insects in the
bayou. Sun buzzing. "Let me give it to you at last, Dad. . . ."*
My hips thrust up. Joe stepped it up. My God, if he only
knew. . . .
Go away. But he wouldn't.
*My father stands up and comes around behind me. Stands me
up. Opens my pants and lets them drop around my thighs. Chair legs
scrape over the linoleum. Works it into me.*
With a groan, I shot all over myself, chest, face, all over
the pillow. Opened my eyes. Joe's face, curious, above me.
"Wow," he said.
I told him about my fantasy. "Outrageous," he said. I
was very happy, if embarrassed.

▲

Joe lay with his eyes closed, hands behind his head, legs
ajar, while I jacked his cock—long, rather flexible, a real
handful. At one point he opened his eyes and I thought he'd
pick up his porno, but he didn't. He turned his head to one
side and I smiled at him, holding his balls in one hand. He
tossed his head again and I asked, *à la* Mayor Koch, "How'm
I doin'?" "Do the head more," he replied, and closed his
eyes.
He opened his legs further and they began to quiver. I
smiled to myself, thinking of the dildo he'd bought (good
old *Joy of Gay Sex*) to "practice" with and get to know his
asshole. He is incredibly industrious, I thought. And as I
was thinking of the applications he'd been filling out for Pan
Am and Eastern—what a scrumptious steward he'd make—
he heaved and came, a monster orgasm that almost didn't
happen—there was a pulse, a pause, then he came.
I whistled. He opened his eyes. His mouth was agape.
His eyes shone with that primordial, postorgastic glaze.
"We get the prize," I said. I'd cum too.
"Oh, really?" he said. Immediately downplaying it.
Mustn't hope too much.

A

Virgil congratulated us, "Though I know you'll probably use your success as an excuse to worry about the next
time."

He's very pleased with us. "You might be interested to
know now," he said, "that all the literature says retarded
ejaculation is the hardest thing to cure. That it takes at least
six months before the patient will ejaculate. . . ." (Well, it felt
like six years.) "That those who suffer from it are invariably
angry people, which you two aren't, and that it has to do
with resentment"—he looked at me—"toward the mother."

I laughed. Virgil smiled. We both knew it had nothing
to do with my mother. Or my real father, for that matter.
But with the Father of my childhood and adolescence, who
hadn't been able to love me. Or me, him. That the issue was
one of giving, nurturing.

A

"What did you want from Max?" Virgil asked, somewhat after the dust had settled and I was getting my bear-
ings in my new apartment.

"It killed me because he had a career and I didn't," I
said. "I was happy for him but jealous."

"Was there something more?"

"I don't know," I said, weary with my need to blame
myself for what had gone wrong, frustrated that I could
find no way to blame Max.

"Did he remind you of anyone?"

"That's interesting," I said, for I'd just thought of
something that Max and I both used to do—a little habit we
shared, of thoughtfully pulling our earlobes when we were
distracted, and the way Max used to rub his lower lip,
something I do, too. And that my father does those things.

"Not my father," I said. "Until the end, when he ig-
nored me. Turned his back on me." I was lightly beating the

chair arm with the side of my hand, trying to figure something out. "A family," I said. "I wanted a family. . . ."

▲

We walked out of the office in silence. My mother's face
was strained and my father held her arm, something he'd
seldom done. Courtly, protective gestures were not in his
line, and she was a most independent person. . . .

I was in an agony of suspense. They'd been in there
with the psychiatrist for half an hour. Whether I'd be allowed to go back to school that fall hung in the balance. I was
in my sophomore year of college and I'd fucked everything
up.

We got into the car. I sat in the back seat, my parents in
the front. My father drove.

We drove down the tree-lined boulevard. It was high
summer and hot.

"What'd he say?" I finally managed to ask.

"He says you should go back to school," my father
answered.

Silence then.

"He says that's the best thing for you," my mother said.
"That you're—you've always been too dependent—on me.
I have to give you up." Her voice was strained, straining at
normalcy.

I'd been able to tell, even from my elementary little
psych course, what the tests were indicating—those cartoon
families, those blobs, those innocent-sounding questions.

"I want to go back to school," I said.

So she let me go.

▲

Thinking of my father, now dying of cancer. Who
wasn't there. Max, who wasn't there.

▲

A few years ago the tapes began to arrive. No fanfare. My father just thought I'd like to know a thing or two about him.

I remember *his* father once thought *he'd* like to know a thing or two, and so sat in his armchair telling my father stories of the prairie, outlaws, life on the range—until he went crazy; then, in his hospital bed, began to live them out. . . .

Retired from work now, with time on his hands, my father begins to write. There was a time, in the midst of the Depression, before he met my mother, when my father tried to write—short stories for the *Saturday Evening Post*, as a means to support his parents. Nothing came of that. Eventually he was able to find other work, with his hands, and he has not stopped working with his hands until now.

In the evenings he sits in his basement study (my old room, where I used to sleep, where I used to hide and dream) and he speaks into a tape recorder, the story of his life.

It takes several drafts, my mother tells me. First by hand, then on the typewriter, pecking out the letters. Then he reads it onto tape.

Grown up, fled to this distant city—as far away, in fact, as I could fly—ironically I've brought the family name back to its source. My parents' folks came from here generations ago. Here was the source of generation upon obscure generation of wanderers. Now I end the generations here.

And now my father, who has spoken perhaps a dozen sentences directly to me, Danny, in the past dozen years, begins to send me tapes of the story of his life.

Meekly at first, full of self-disparagement. The preface alone is a masterpiece of procrastination and digression. He can't remember it all, he says, not near enough. He's not an educated man. It wasn't much of a life. But he thought I'd like to know a thing or two.

I sit listening to a voice I've never heard before, wondering, Why me? Why now? This stranger, insinuating himself into my life.

The old wolf limps back to the cave, looking for a warm place to lay his head. The ogre returns to the castle, storms about, cries out for music.

When people sit around swapping stories about their childhoods, I draw a blank, especially about him. Methodically, I've put him out of my mind; that morose man without hope, that silent stranger who slept odd hours and ate alone at our table, that unblinking eye watching over all my failures and foolishness. But my amnesia was only a clumsy camouflage. His absence was more powerful than was his presence.

In the dark hall a terrible encephalitic skull hangs above the throne. Thunder and lightning. But with a sigh a screen falls to the slate floor, revealing in the shadows a frightened little man.

My father moved through our house like the vacuum nature abhors, sucking up all the fragile barriers we placed in his path. His absence echoed with my first tentative steps. Even present, he was a deep black well my mother's prattle dropped into like pebbles.

When people sit around talking about their childhoods, *their* fathers, I remember nothing but a few bitter details: the baseball burning into my outstretched palms, the bicycle left disassembled on the garage floor, the yardstick kept in readiness for the foreordained whipping.

Then the tapes begin to arrive.

He calls them "Vignettes of a Small Town," as if the Nebraska town alone were of any interest. He styles himself a small-town boy, and his voice—soft, drawling—confirms it.

There is a piecemeal genealogy: the obligatory courtship of father and mother, the births of sisters and brothers.

His own arrival on the scene is a modest footnote; he is most obsessed with the lay of the land, the ponderously turning seasons, the press of History.

And I think, This is what he was born to do, to write.

But I think, No, I'm not like him, I'm not.

One night in June, I sit in my apartment listening to my

father sing for me, in a voice I've never heard, the song played on the calliope in the circus parade down Main Street. He remembers all the words.

Down in the basement, his memory burgeons painfully. Though the cancer hasn't yet exploded in his loins, each death of each loved one is a premonition of his own, every word of the story of his life throbs with the knowledge he is dying. He rushes on to tell it.

Jokes, gossip, tall tales, slander and scandal—he remembers and relates them all. He describes the drift of cottonseed in a sludge along the margins of a stream; the delicious nausea of the first forbidden cigarette; the exact placement of ranks and ranks of jars on the cellar shelves. In his quavering new voice—tight with emotion, tight with decorum—he tells the story of his life.

And I think, His love is reaching out to me.

But I think, I do not love him, I won't be forced to love him now.

About his father: he is kind to the old man, who likewise wasn't there, busy making sure he'd set foot in each of the forty-eight states, busy trading horses, real estate.

About his mother: he guesses *he* was a mama's boy, too worshipful, too sensitive to suit his dad.

The tapes keep arriving.

My mother told him to come back when he wasn't drunk.

What kind of man was he, he asked himself during the Depression, who had to board his own daughter with strangers.

About the others: miscarried; aborted; the elusive, obsessive idea of a son.

And I think, I won't listen any longer, to what I was meant to be, wasn't.

Fervently prayed for, born late, determined to murder myself in the womb.

I am born and grow up in my father's eyes.

A

The Fourth of July. I am five years old. My father has sunk a pipe in concrete in the front yard, for a flagpole—a little dream of his. In the morning he calls me to come outside with him. He takes the folded flag out of the bottom drawer of the desk. He hands it to me, admonishes me to hold it tight, not to drop it.

Then I, carrying the flag, and he, carrying the flagpole (how rotten and splintered it will get in the years to come), walk across the dewy grass to the center of the yard, where the flagpole will stand flanked by tiny maple trees (how gigantic they'll grow until one is split in two by an ice storm).

Picking out the grommeted corners of the flag I hold in my arms, my father then lashes the flag to the flagpole. He tells me to hold up the corners of the flag; it would be sacrilege for the holy flag to touch the ground (and, oh, how I believe him, how watching the flag burned before my eyes by friends, so many years later, made me ache).

He lifts the flagpole. The corners of the flag slip out of my hands. He urges the butt end of the flagpole into the mouth of the pipe.

Then he shows me how to stand straight-backed, hand on heart, saluting the flag.

A silver airplane flies overhead. A breeze catches the flag and stirs it. Children are screaming, running in and out of lawn sprinklers, up and down the street. My father's sober face hovers above me. The sun shines down on my blond hair. My father's hand descends to my shoulder. He squeezes my shoulder, then he takes me up in his arms and carries me back into the house.

And I think, Were there ever times like these? In whose life?

But the voice on the tape says there were, limns them in precious detail, caresses them, and hesitates, clears its throat, vibrates with pride and loss.

▲

"Danny!" exclaims my sister. "What a surprise! Is anything wrong?"

"No, nothing's wrong. Can't I call my sister without anything being wrong?"

"It's Saturday night."

"Am I interrupting anything?"

"No, we were just out in the back yard."

"How are you?"

"You sound strange."

"Well, I feel a little strange. I've just been listening to Dad's tape. . . ."

"I got mine this morning," she says.

"It's made me feel a little strange."

"How—strange?"

"I've been dreaming about him."

"Oh."

"How are you?" I ask again.

"What's wrong with you, Danny?"

"I don't understand. It's like a whole other life. I don't remember anything he's describing."

"Well, I was older," she says after a pause. "And you know, I think—you're going to laugh at this."

"No I won't."

"I think you were always his favorite. Not me, after all."

"But he—"

"After a certain point, he never held you on his lap. He didn't kiss you or hold you. Is that what you mean?"

"Yes."

▲

I remember a snapshot of him I used to study, in the pile of snapshots my mother kept in the bureau drawer, a snapshot of him as a young man, in his uniform.

I asked if Daddy was in the army.

"No, the CCC's," my mother said. "Doing work for the government. Your Daddy built dams. It was the Depression."

She held up the snapshot and looked at it.

"This is right after we met," she said. "Wasn't your father a handsome man?"

Was I searching for that face on the New York streets? A face that seemed somehow familiar? Those downcast eyes? That grim mouth?

I look in the mirror. Oh God, I've become him.

&

"Don't you realize?" says my actor friend. "Your father's giving you a tremendous legacy. The story of his life."

"It's too late."

"It's not what you wanted," he says. "He's loving you the way *he* can, not the way you wanted."

&

"We went to pick up Danny at summer camp. But we'd forgotten to tell him to look after his lips. You see, like me, my son has lips that are easily sunburned. When we got to the camp, there was Danny, just a little boy, and his lips were cracked and blistered from the sun. No one had looked after him and told him to put something on his lips, to protect them.

"He was barefoot, standing next to his pup tent. He was dirty and sunburned. I looked at those lips and I said to my wife, 'God, no one told him to take care of his lips. Look how blistered they are.'

" 'Shh,' my wife said. 'His little friends will hear you.' They were all standing around waiting for their parents.

"I walked over to him and asked him if he was packed and he said yes. He'd rolled everything up in his sleeping bag, in a big wad. 'We can't go yet,' he said, saying they had to sign out.

"So we stood there and I felt like a fool. I wanted to kneel down and take that poor little boy in my arms, due to his blistered lips and his terrible sunburn. But I didn't as I didn't want to embarrass him in front of his friends."

⚑

"I just want someone to hold me," says one of the men in my therapy group.

"The only time my father touched me was to hit me," says another.

"We used to fight all the time, but when I got old enough I beat him up," says another.

"My father slammed the door in my face."

"My father turned his back on me and told me to leave."

"My father knocked me down."

"My father just laughed."

"My father wouldn't listen."

"My father kept reading his newspaper."

"My father left me alone after that."

"My mother wrote that he was dead."

⚑

I have a composer friend who lives in an apartment high above Park Avenue. My childhood dream of New York always incorporated such an apartment. A penthouse with a baby grand piano set against a backdrop of city lights. And in many ways an evening with my composer friend is a fulfillment of those childhood fantasies.

Some of us went up there one night. It was hazy out, so there was no sharp-edged brilliance to the skyline, but the Empire State Building shone in its own luminescent cocoon and the traffic lights on Park Avenue glowed green then red, like landing lights in the fog.

It was a small dinner party, cooked by my friend himself. He's a gourmand and this is the only entertaining he does. ("So exquisitely mounted," my novelist friend whispered when we saw the table.)

But there are no pretensions about an evening with

him. After years of just such dinners, his manner as a host is completely casual. He tells us stories of the great, the near-great, their lovers. He's never, in my presence at least, repeated any one of those stories. The fund of them seems endless.

He's in his fifties now and was "once a great beauty," as my novelist friend confided long ago—as if true beauty couldn't mutate and alter itself with age. Since he didn't, evidently, *use* his beauty, his success as a composer came as a surprise to those in circles where beauty was an ornament and its own eventual punishment.

He has lots of stories to tell about gay life as it used to be on the "Bird Circuit," those bars in the Fifties on the East Side, in Provincetown, abroad. For me, the penthouse exists in a time warp of obscure origin, high above the avenue and far away from the mean streets where most of us live. My political friend wasn't comfortable there, nor was I initially. One's own identity inevitably takes on an impalpability there. You have to stop for a moment, once back down on the pavement, to gather yourself up before you're ready to walk on.

That night we stood around the piano after dinner and my friend played Gershwin, because I'd begged him to. Then he played some of his own compositions late into the night. When the others had gone and his own lover had said good night, my friend broke out the brandy and we sat on a banquette sipping our drinks and talking.

I was drunk, and fascinated by the beauty of my friend's profile against the skyline. Warmed by the glow of the candles he'd set out on the cocktail table before us, his face was translucent. Backlit by the tall chrome lamp in the corner, his hair glowed on the helmet of his skull. I wanted to place my hands on that skull, perhaps to read it like a phrenologist, perhaps to capture some of the vitality that seemed to radiate from him.

"Do you mind?" I asked, and shifted my weight on the banquette, lay with my head in his lap.

His hand came to rest on my stomach. I could feel the words vibrating in his chest before I heard them.

He talked on into the dawn. The haze over the city slid from blue-gray to pink. I drifted in and out of inattention as I picked up this string or that of his long story, let it slip through my fingers, drift off. Then I slept.

He awakened me with a kiss on the lips, soft, and then his soft tongue entered my mouth. I opened my eyes. His eyes, too, were open on mine. They contained some element of playfulness, some element of confusion.

He broke the kiss. His fingers patted my ribs once or twice.

"I didn't expect that," I said.

"I wanted to kiss you."

"I'm sorry," I said.

"Nothing more."

"I know."

I sat up. He stretched a bit. "It's way past *your* bedtime," he said. (He never seems to sleep.) He unbent his legs again.

"Yeah," I said. I rose.

He showed me to the door. I thanked him and, after giving me a hug, he said, "What *is* it you think you wanted?"

I didn't know.

A

Once when I came in for an appointment alone with Virgil, he gave me a pad of drawing paper and a pencil, asked me to draw some pictures. At the top of the first sheet was the caption "me."

From my elementary psych course, I knew what this was all about. I suppose I might have even sneered a bit. But I sat down and drew a picture of myself. A piece of cake, I thought. I was bound up, with ropes, on my knees, head swathed in bandages.

I couldn't resist saying to him, when I'd finished, "Pretty obvious, isn't it?"

"Go on," he said.

I flipped over the top sheet. On the next page the caption said, "my family."

I began drawing. I drew a bench. On the bench were two shrouded figures with their backs to the viewer. But their faces were turned to the front. Each was indistinguishable from the other. Next to them, standing facing me, was a nude woman. She was smiling. I sketched in a landscape of sorts. A twisted tree sat at the top of a low, bare hill.

"What have you drawn?" Virgil asked when I sat down in the chair next to him.

I described the picture.

"You left yourself out of the family," he said.

"Yes. I suppose I did. I feel that way."

"Who is the naked woman?"

"My sister. She likes me."

"And the others?"

"My father and mother, like I said."

"Which is which?"

I pointed to each figure in turn, realizing, of course, that they were really sexless.

"Take the picture home with you," Virgil said, "and look at it when you get some time. See if anything else occurs to you about it."

So I did. And the next time I went to see Virgil, I told him what had impressed me about the sketch when I looked at it that night.

"That they're all—except for my sister—suspicious and, somehow, pained. They're in pain. As they're rejecting me, with their backs turned. But also something else."

"What's that?"

"The landscape. I realized what the picture should be called. 'Depression.' The literal Depression—they told me about it time and time again, all the time I was growing up, their sacrifices and their trials. Horror stories, really. And also just plain depression. What I'm in the middle of now. That life is depression and their lot is mine. And one more thing."

"What?"

"That that's what my father taught me, because he was an unhappy man and. . . ."

He waited for me to complete the sentence.

"I loved him. He taught me to be depressed. I didn't think he'd taught me anything, that I wasn't part of him. But it's *all* him. Don't you think? My father drew the picture, not me."

▲

The day I became a man, I rushed home from the office and packed a suitcase. I put on a suit and a black tie. I took a cab to the airport. Several hours later, I was in my father's hospital room.

The air conditioning hissed in the baseboards. The blinds were drawn against the twilight. My mother stood at the foot of the bed.

My father lay with a tube in his nose. His hands lay at his sides, on top of the sheets. He was sleeping.

I kissed my mother and we held each other tight. "He came out of it real well," she whispered.

He awakened briefly. I leaned over him. I kissed my father's dry forehead. His eyes were vacant, but not from the anesthetic. His eyes were vacant from fear. The pupils were dilated. He blinked. " . . .here," he said. "Thank you for coming here."

And I, frozen in my own strait jacket of emotion, managed to touch his hand. I put my fingers on the back of his hand. He closed his eyes.

Not yet, I thought, you won't die yet.

At home, in my parents' house, I took off my suit jacket, took off the black tie. My mother served us dinner, pausing every once in a while in the kitchen, forgetting where things were, forgetting what she'd put on the stove.

"Can't I help you?" I asked.

"No," she said. "No, I have to keep busy."

I put my head down on the table and cried.

When I left the next week, my mother called my sister and told her what a help I'd been, that I'd become a man.

⚠

A brief reprieve they chose to pretend (what else was there for them to do?) was permanent.

"I was shocked. I was stunned. I loved him," I told my therapy group. "But I was disappointed. . . ."

Why?

"That he didn't—that he didn't die."

At least one of them was sickened when I said that.

The doctor said a year. Two years.

⚠

"After a certain point," my sister says, "he never held you on his lap. He didn't kiss you or hold you. Is that what you mean?"

"Yes."

"Well, he couldn't. You understand?"

"Yes."

"But he loved you. Little boys love their mothers, little girls love their fathers. It took me a long time before Mom and I were friends."

"Yes."

"But it's more complicated with you."

"Yes."

"You just cut him off." A pause. "Didn't you?"

"Yes." The tears are streaming down my face, but I don't let on.

To Flamingo with my dancing friend. In his circle there are not four seasons in New York but two—summer and winter. So we go there tonight to celebrate that arbitrary solstice that marks the return from the Island to the City. Arbitrary, too, is the night Michael has chosen to reopen Flamingo. For it is a Thursday night, and the fact that we have come here on "a school night," as my friend puts it, immediately certifies our freedom from the standards of the mundane.

We meet at his little hovel on Horatio Street. There is no ceiling left in the living room. It fell down long ago. And the bathroom is so disgraceful that my feminist friend—even she—refuses to use it. But my dancing friend is waiting for me, a steaming cup of coffee in his hand, neat as a pin in oft-laundered duds, his professional garb of V-neck T-shirt, corduroys with the wale rubbed away fore and aft, Adidas.

The hour of our meeting is arbitrary, too. For we are to arrive early (1:00 A.M.) even though it is not, as my friend frets, "fashionable or prudent." The really good music (to his admittedly rarified taste) won't be played until six.

"If you go on time, you have to contend with the crowd

scene at the coat check. If you go too early, you get the Top Forty."

But Flamingo always leaves me saucer-eyed at whatever hour. To me the difference between one thousand half-naked men dancing their asses ragged and two or three thousand is academic. And whatever might be coming out of those gigantic speakers is beside the point, given the visuals.

Never in the history of the male physique, not even on the playing fields of Sparta, have there been such perfect tits and asses. Never in the annals of Nebuchadnezzar, Assurbanipal, or Tiglath-Pileser were there recorded such scenes of (relatively) unbridled revelry. Never in my life have I known such (relative) out-of-body travel as I've known at Flamingo. Under any other circumstances, Flamingo would be my idea of the myth of Tantalus rewritten for the modern age. But now I can't have sex anyway.

This is a private club, or else it wouldn't be able to exist as it is—the special preserve of a tidy one thousand and their friends, that special cross-section of muscle queens and style queens endemic to Island society. But the limited membership is only one aspect of the illusion of elitism that gives Flamingo its cachet (among those who care for such things). Camouflaged outwardly by its location in a nondescript warehouse building on the edge of Lower Manhattan, furnished with nothing more elaborate than industrial gray wall-to-wall carpeting, a few platforms, a vast highly-polished dance floor, those gigantic speakers of course, and banks and banks of lights, Flamingo is the height of reverse-chic.

Flamingo is masquerading as itself tonight. Tangerine and lime palm trees are projected onto the white walls. There are none of the decorative excesses that distinguish the White and Black parties, no hunky models perched on platforms in laser-sharp downlight, no elaborate S&M psychodramas, no X-rated slide shows featuring the head of James Dean superimposed onto the body of the Cobra Woman.

There are rented limos parked outside at the curb. The staff is arrayed in tuxes at the door, checking off the members and checking out the new list for the new year. Miscreants and no-shows have been deleted, promising newcomers welcomed aboard. Champagne is being served.

One thousand is a cozy number: everyone seems to know everyone else. My dancing friend says "hiya" to bobbing heads on either side of us as we make our progress to the juice bar, where he will permit himself one single glass of club soda. (In matters of dance he is, it should be clear, an ascetic, eschews even the aid of drugs.)

There is a deceptive sobriety to the lounge, which is separated from the dance floor by a mirrored wall. Some of us stand talking; many more stand watching; all are out to see who has survived the transition from Summer Person to this more rigorous indoor context. Each of us stands in a spotlight of his own devising. It is as if the radiant egos of summer have been turned in upon themselves. Eyes smolder, but the rest is surface, a subtly pulsating frieze of flesh, still mat, not yet glistening with sweat.

A deceptive sobriety, because the two wide doors to the dance floor are portals to a cyclorama that might have been etched by Doré. It is in many respects like a scene out of the *Purgatorio*. For that dance floor, that pedestrian square of parquet, is situated directly between the *Inferno* of "real life" and the *Paradiso* we've all come here to achieve. On the right night, with the right drugs and the right music, a membership card to Flamingo can be a visa to a disembodied and transcendent state, beyond the Iron Curtain of individual identity, through a looking glass of ego, into the Land of Nod.

My dancing friend notes the refurbishments. The overhead light wall has been moved to the Great Divide. Michael has opened up the back room to the dance floor. But otherwise, my friend (who hates change, who hates the New Music) is satisfied.

"I used to love to kiss Frank Miller in that back room," he sighs. "It was the only physical contact we ever had. One night he asked me out on the stairs for a blowjob, and it completely ruined our relationship."

So much for the back room.

I am satisfied, too. I have no idea whatsoever who Frank Miller is and no one at Flamingo has ever asked me out on the stairs for a blowjob. No one is likely to. I am safe.

Suddenly, it is four o'clock in the morning and I am high as a kite. My Fire Island friend—glimpsed briefly over the heads and shoulders of the dancers—dancing on one of the bleachers that runs the length of the room, then encountered later in the john, has given me some unspecified drug.

"What will it do to me?" I gasped, as he took it out of its foil envelope and popped it into my mouth.

"Take you up. You look a little peaked."

And it took me up.

Several times my dancing friend, who relates only to his own rhythms, who charts only his own moves, has danced in front of me, put a reassuring hand on my shoulder and (through a veil of shattering prisms) has looked deep into my eyes, just like Doctor Dan the Bandage Man.

But now I am more like myself (more's the pity), and the beat of the music doesn't solely have its source in my groin. I'm at least conscious that there are other people on the floor—elbowing me in the ribs, stepping on my feet, passing poppers hand to hand, spraying ethyl into the air as if it were *Eau de Nuit*.

Crowded. *Everyone* is here. But not so crowded that I don't spot a man standing not far from us, on the edge of the floor, looking at me, clapping his hands along with the beat, smiling. I smile back, but embarrassed by his unwavering cruise (at Flamingo, of all places), I steer myself around so I'm not directly facing him.

He moves, and soon I'm looking into his eyes again. Even the pulsating lights and shadows on the dance floor don't obscure the amusement, interest, and—oh, Jesus— intelligence in his eyes. He is obviously a mirage.

I take another hit of amyl.

He's still there.

Perhaps forty, great build, salt-and-pepper hair cut short, the obligatory mustache. And that face. Not the cattle-prod-jolt-to-the-balls face, but the "I am Gatsby, won't you join me on my yacht for a cool drink" face.

So it's a fantasy. I may be stuck with Daddy for a while, but I'll be damned if I have to take on Alan Ladd too.

There is a sheen on his $250 Sheridan Square Health Club chest. There are those straight white teeth. There is the unremitting, ironic cruise.

What with the whatever-it-was my Fire Island friend gave me and the poppers, I am slow to admit that this is what I want. Yes. Now. Him. This great corporeal manifestation of a wet dream.

He is dancing with us now, I have a silly, senior-prom grin on my face, and my stomach is flopping. I wonder what the fuck I'm going to do with this gorgeous man who is— yes— interested in me, running his palms over my chest.

In me. Danny Slocum.

Ever mindful of my social obligations, I offer him the popper bottle. He shakes his head no thanks. I take another hit and put the bottle into my back pocket. My dancing friend is intensely involved in this byplay. I know because he is elaborately pretending not to be. As he spins around, he shoots me a look that says, Your round, Miss Thing, and dances away.

Don't leave me! You know I can't have sex!

("What will you tell him? 'I'm in sex therapy and can't have sex with you'?")

The amyl rush hits back, but it brings me down more than it pumps me up. Somehow my drugs have gotten "discontoured." I am desperately *here* with this man—who is unreal in the first place, but, shit, so real, so downright three-dimensional, caressing my nipples, fingers running down my belly.

Think of something! Don't just swoon!

"Wanna take a break?" I pant, desperate for some
strategy to get Mr. X into my bed—bed, hell, into my shower—sometime, sometime in the future.

"What?"

I repeat my ploy.

"Naw," he says. "I think I'll dance with my friends."

He weaves away through the crowd.

Who are your friends? Are they friends of friends?

I am down now, all the way down.

As I pull on my flannel shirt, yank on my jacket, put my
glasses on, button up and slog out into the dawn, I think,
Romance-shromance. I won't let this happen again.

ʌ

Halloween evening. After leaving me, Joe drives down
Christopher Street. (Destination, dirty bookstore, to buy a
new dildo. This after Virgil's warning that the one he'd
bought on Long Island, having no "balls," might get lost up
his ass. Practice.) Or *trying* to drive down Christopher Street.
There is an enormous crowd on the street, masked and
costumed (oh, yes, much like any other night) in a festive,
whacko mood.

A zonked-out transvestite is stopping cars, or rather,
assaulting their occupants with attitude and good humor
while they stand stranded in the traffic jam.

Joe is three or four cars back from the TV and the knot
of people who surround her and the car whose hood she
dances on. A man in a black Stetson stops, does a double
take at Joe, smirks, cups his basket, and settles in for a long
cruise.

Joe is rather liking it—the attention of the cowboy, who
has now gotten quite verbal about it, the carnival swirling
around his car, even sweating out his turn with the TV.

The cars inch forward. Men, men, men flow around
Joe like water around a ship's prow. Some smile, some give
him the dead-eye cruise (pretending not to notice, saying,
"Look at me, eatcha heart out"), some stop and lean against

his car. His fenders are being polished by a dozen Levied butts! What attention!

And from being so out of it, so Long Island, so down— he is suddenly *in it*, right smack dab in the middle of it, a million miles from Korvettes and his room with the dumb-bells and the closet mirror, the porno hidden beneath his underwear in the drawer, his mother's silent questions as he slips out the door.

He has told me this and I've wanted to take him in my arms, for this is what he's been moving toward. Not the Christopher Street carnival, not a stranger's denim *tushe*, but this sudden sense, this rush of freedom, this glimpse of a future.

&

We are wary. It's working and we don't want to rock the boat. I complain to Virgil that we're too involved with this. Like Joe, I feel that this is again sucking up the rest of my life, and I've brought too much of myself into it for comfort.

"But that's just it," Virgil says, smiling.

"What?"

"To put yourself in it."

I sit back and think while Joe is talking. Yes, to put myself in it. I was trying to fuck with all those guys just like they tell you to do in the porno magazines, or like we assume you have to be able to in the decade of the zipless fuck. Keeping myself out of it, though my body was in it. And the body said no.

&

Joe kneels between my legs. With a look on his face of curiosity mingled with distaste, he takes my cock in his mouth. A flutter. Then he is off and jacking it with his fingers again. A pause. He lifts the glass of water to his lips and takes two or three sips, then goes down on me again.

None of this has been prescribed by Virgil, this sipping and jerking, hand to mouth, so to speak. He has not sucked cock much and when he has, he's been heavily face-fucked, the last time by some dude in the back seat of a Ford Pinto.

I have billed myself as a terrific cocksucker. Joe has not been persuaded.

We are not angry people. We *are* fearful people (the flip side). Fearful, complicating—paranoid? Fearful of coercion. Fearful of unleashing dark forces within ourselves. Fearful of this act with all its mythology and its associations. We can't feel it.

Flutter-flutter. Sip-sip. Tuggings, scrapings, tonguings, warmth, coolness—all vague, pastel, not red-hot. I'm shy again about giving instructions.

I go down on Joe. "Um-humph?" Hard to ask questions with your mouth packed full of cock.

We jack each other off. I cum first (old hat), then Joe. And when he cums it is—well, weird. That familiar pulse, the beat before he cums, is elongated into two, three, four pulses. When he cums it is an almost-not.

"Weird," I say.

"What do you mean?"

"You mean you didn't feel it?"

"What?"

"It was as if you almost didn't cum."

"Well I *did*."

"What's wrong?"

"Fuck you." (From under the arm he's thrown over his face.)

"What's wrong?"

I rub his belly.

"Stop it. I can hide if I want to."

I leave him lying there and go pee. He wanted to be praised and petted. So I lie down beside him, praise and pet him a bit.

In the shower we both agree we're tired and pressured. We feel weepy. Blowing. Joe has a lot to learn and I a lot to unlearn. Same thing. Whenever this happens, this lack of progress, each of us blames the other.

⚠

At Virgil's suggestion, Joe has been practicing blowing—whether with a cucumber or his dildo, he won't tell me. "How's it going?" I ask over the phone.

"Now I have to practice cocksucking," he says, exasperated. "I have to practice putting a dildo up my ass to get fucked. I have to suck on a cucumber to learn how to cocksuck. I have to practice filling out employment applications for my group therapy. I have to practice dancing in front of the mirror to see how my ass looks at the disco. If everyone had to practice as much as I do, there wouldn't be any homosexuals."

⚠

We try different positions. Virgil says our necks might be tense, that we might not feel in control in certain positions, that we will learn how to breathe better in due time. Practice, practice. Neither one of us gets at all close to cumming. Joe is getting pretty good. . . .

⚠

I have moved down to the Village (!).

It happened very fast. Just when my old lease was running out and I was in a financial panic as usual, my curator friend called and asked if I knew anyone who wanted to sublet. He's moving to Baltimore for a couple of years but wants to use the apartment every once in a while, so we've worked out this deal. . . .

And here I am.

I bribed the landlord to get out of my old lease, called up the movers, spent a frantic few days packing, transferring the phone, electric, etc. And here I am.

Tonight Joe and I "practiced" in the bedroom of my new apartment, surrounded by a wall of boxes.

I feel as if *I'm* the one who moved to Baltimore. This is like another city. My novelist friend is very pleased, though he's too discreet under the circumstances to repeat his promise that living down here will revolutionize my sex life.

The Johnson brothers moved me again. They remembered the other two moves, in with Max and out. "Oh, this is *much* nicer," said the elder Mr. Johnson when I let them into my new apartment.

And it is. There is air and light and I'm living in the Village and I have a bedroom and a living room and a kitchen and they're all separated by doors.

Joe is pleased, too. (If a bit intimidated; he had to give his name to the doorman tonight.) He brought a bottle of wine to celebrate and we had a glass or two before "practice." Before he left, he turned to me and said, "I wish you all the best. This is very nice."

I thanked him.

"Will you still talk to me when this is over?" he asked.

"What do you mean?"

"Now that you've moved to the Village and all."

I put my arms around him and hugged him. He hugged me back.

"What do you suppose *will* happen when we finish?" I asked.

"We'll have lunch?" He gave me a squeeze.

He's always afraid I'll leap ahead or pull away, but I'm sure when this *is* over that I'll want to see him more than he'll want to see me: he'll want to put it all behind him.

A

Housewarming last night. I invited people and they in turn brought people and it was a great party. Joe came with a Long Island friend who's just moved into the City himself. The friend was very gregarious, but Joe kept him in a corner most of the evening. I introduced Joe to some of my friends. They'd been carefully coached not to mention our "practice" together. But I don't think Joe would have minded. He looked terrific.

I saw everything through a light Valium haze. ("And not a drop of booze," said my Fire Island friend. "Tonight you're Loretta Young, not Bette Davis.")

When Max and I had finished painting our new apartment, we had a housewarming, too, and invited all our friends. It was my idea. I suppose a lot of the blame for our ill-advised move can be placed squarely on my shoulders, but only with the advantage of hindsight. In any case, it was my idea to have the party. I wanted to announce it. A big punctuation mark (:). Last night I felt I had something else to announce. But the results aren't, of course, in yet.

"Where'd you get all the new friends?" my political friend asked at one point, looking at the crowded room. I put my arm around him. "I don't know," I said. "Isn't it nice?"—remembering my misanthropic post-Max days.

⚐

Joe reports he had a good time at the party, though he didn't understand half of what my novelist friend was driving at or what the argument (?) was about between my political friend and my dancing friend. He thought my actor friend was dreamy and was disappointed when I told him he had a lover. I assured him, though, that my actor friend probably *was* cruising him, if only as a matter of courtesy, and found Joe dreamy, too. Joe was quite disconcerted that my Fire Island friend, after a few minutes of conversation, said, "Oh, *the* Joe." But then they both got to talking and agreed that I was "coming along just fine."

⚐

There aren't *that* many more gay men on my street down here than there were uptown. But there *are* a lot of N.Y.U. students of indeterminate age and sexual persuasion, boys who give you long, ambiguous stares, then hitch up their rucksacks and their jeans and lope away.

⚨

The argument between my dancing friend and my political friend was over Donna Summer versus Gloria Gaynor for the title of Disco Queen!

I threw out a lot of old files today, *Playbills*, the philosophy 301 term papers, the souvenirs of Max. . . .

⚨

We seem to be on the same schedule. He's walking his dog when I leave for work in the mornings and I've seen him in the grocery store two Saturdays running. Twice, when Joe and I had driven down from Virgil's and were going in for "practice," I saw him walking the dog again, and noted the time.

When this is over—should I buy a dog?

⚨

Tonight, I thought Joe was going to cum. His legs trembled and I stepped it up a bit. But then he sighed and put his fingers under my chin to urge me off.

"I thought you were going to cum there."

"No. It was your teeth. They hurt."

Sorry. Wrong number.

⚨

Tonight, I asked Joe to put his finger up my ass. He did. But nothing.

"Maybe I should bring my dildo," he suggested.

"I don't know," I said (wondering why I'm so reluctant to "practice" as he does). "Wouldn't it be sort of like sharing a toothbrush?" I quipped.

"You're very condescending sometimes," he said. I agreed with him. I am. He very sweetly forgave me. He'll do that when he's made his point.

⚑

This morning I stepped out into the sunshine and gave *him* a cheery hello. He was rather taken aback and the dog wrapped its leash around his legs. But he managed to return my greeting.

⚑

My political friend called the other day and asked a long series of questions about slow cumming, to an extent that I was about to satisfy my suspicion that it was his problem, too. But it wasn't. He's been seeing this guy. . . .

I told him to sit cross-legged facing his friend and that the two of them should jack each other off, then when he felt the other guy wasn't/was about to cum, just take his hand and indicate he was to do himself. Then give him a big kiss. "As soon as you give him permission to bring himself off, he might be able to relax and do it." He thanked me for the advice. "But for godsake," I added, "don't talk to him about it, just do it."

He called today. It worked!

⚑

I remember telling Virgil once that my Fire Island friend had suggested I go to the Glory Hole, where there's nothing but a series of booths with holes you can stick your dong through to get blown, etc. Virgil laughed. "A lot of guys go to back-room places like the Glory Hole and the Mineshaft," he said, "as if they want to put their dysfunctions on display. A public, pressured scene. It's the last place for you."

Yet my Fire Island friend is thoroughly relaxed at the Glory Hole. It works for him.

I wonder if after this is over I'll need an hour of getting-to-know-you over tea and cakes, a warm shower, and a massage before I'm even ready to *begin* to function.

When my Fire Island friend and I are walking on the street, deep in conversation, and I miss an especially pretty ass or face—he misses *nothing*—he looks at me as if he's the Pope and I've just spit on the cross. . . .

◭

"You know," said Joe last night, resting his head on my thigh, "this blowing is very boring."

"Maybe that's why we aren't cumming," I said.

He sat up on the bed and took a swig of Cranapple juice, his new enthusiasm. (At least he isn't slobbering *that* all over my cock; the exotic techniques have gone by the way-side.) He tossed his hair off his forehead.

I traced a finger down his arm. The tan is almost faded out.

"I didn't think *anything* could be more boring than jacking," he said. "I thought that if we blew like we jacked, then we'd cum."

"In the head," I said, tapping my temple.

He fingered the head of my cock.

"It certainly ain't there," he said, looking down at the little winking piss-hole.

◭

"Such emphasis on performance and technique," Virgil said. "You guys know what to do."

But in the meantime, he has this other idea. . . .

◭

I have just had the interesting experience of having my

therapist offer me his lover for sex. I declined. I've known him too long and God knows what it might do to my transference.

But Joe took him up on it, rather liking the idea. "I don't know," he said. "It's kind of like going to bed with *him*."

"You realize what you just said?"

"I don't mean that. I mean he'll get it straight from the horse's mouth now."

Glorioski.

The idea is that we gradually transfer onto other people, the answer to my Fire Island friend's perennial question as to whether Joe and I will be stuck with each other forever. It is now November and we've been doing this since July.

So we should each have a session with a surrogate.

The supply of male sex surrogates, I take it, is quite limited. (*Note: Remember to tell actor friend this is not, repeat, not easy work, and that it takes the dedication of a Salvation Army captain and the patience of a Sister of Charity.*) Virgil's lover is well-trained, I take it, and of course comes highly recommended. . . .

A

Joe appeared at the door at precisely the appointed hour, a little box of pastries in hand, and Virgil went out to see a movie.

They talked about Michael's studies and looked at some of Michael's drawings. ("I have some more in the bedroom.")

Michael suggested they massage each other, and Joe agreed. They took off their clothes. Joe lay down on his back, as he would with me. "How about your back first?" Michael suggested. Joe turned over. Michael didn't use any oil. His touch was light and feathery. At one point he ran the hairs on his arm down Joe's back. Joe shivered, not sure how much he liked it. He realized then he wasn't saying anything. His mind was so full of the admonition to say something, anything, that he couldn't think of what to say.

He turned over and Michael leaned down and licked his nipple. Joe's body jumped a bit. He hadn't expected that at all. Then Michael sat back on his heels and began massaging Joe's thighs. Every once in a while a hand would stray away from the center of Michael's attention to rest on a nipple or a shoulder or next to Joe's balls. Every once in a while, Michael would lightly feel his way around the head of Joe's prick.

Joe just lay passive. Being with Michael was so different from being with me—or anyone else he'd been with, for that matter. He didn't know what was coming next. Inwardly he laughed at himself and his predicament. It wasn't that Michael was in control of the situation, but that they were both drifting toward their destination—Joe's orgasm—without knowing *how* they would arrive there.

Just like real sex.

Joe felt paralyzed. He knew he was supposed to give Michael a hint as to what he wanted him to do, but the words wouldn't come to him.

Michael asked Joe to massage him, and Joe did. Then Michael blew Joe for a while, then jacked and blew him. But Joe couldn't cum. Michael lay down for a rest, his hard cock sticking out from between his slender thighs. He took Joe in his arms and held him, and Joe sighed. He felt the evening was going to be a total washout. He wanted to say, "Oh, Michael"—as he sometimes says "Oh, Danny"—meaning, "What am I going to do?"

"Do you mind if I cum?" Michael asked. And then he jacked himself off.

"It must be very frustrating work," Joe observed.

"Yes, it is," Michael replied.

So Joe said he wanted to jack himself off. He lay back in bed with a new copy of *Mandate* with a hunky guy in it. As he was about to cum, he took Michael's hand, but Michael didn't know Joe wanted him to finish him. Joe came.

They showered and had coffee and the pastries. Virgil

called, asking if he could come home. Joe left before Virgil got there, accepting Michael's congratulations, but feeling mildly depressed about the whole thing.

🔺

"But you came!" I said over the phone.
"Yeah."
Silence.
"Joe, where'd you get that? That never-give-yourself-a-break thing?"
"I don't know."
"From *your* father?"
"Mother, I guess."
"Well, if we're both stuck with it, at least we don't have to act as if we are. *You came.*"
"Yeah. It wasn't real sex."

🔺

Boy, if Sammy wasn't real sex, I don't know what is.
Nonstop talker—Studio 54, his childhood in Brooklyn, his design classes, the shoes he wears to dance in, all the jobs he's had, his girlfriends, his boyfriends—yak yak yak. And all the while steering me through my paces.
I feel like I've just come back to the old homestead from Kansas City. That boy turned me every which way but up. Gave me organs I never knew I had. Played me like a calliope.
"You like that, don't you, you should see yourself there, lying there with that grin on your face, here, put it there, that's it, terrific, that really feels good, let's kiss."
"A cock like that has to have a name," I say.
He hefts it in his hand. "How'd you know? Thumper."
He jacked me every which way but off, blew me every which way but away, and then jacked me up to the Mega-O. Had me screaming. Rolling in the aisles. Then dashed away to catch forty winks before Studio.

⚠

Sammy's report to Virgil: "Very cerebral. Very repressed. I'm surprised he even came."

⚠

And boy, was I in trouble. I knew it even before the door slammed behind Sammy. I would have to tell Joe I had a terrific time.

I downplayed it at Virgil's, but it didn't do any good. In the car, on the way downtown to my place, Joe was silent. At home I bustled around, fixing coffee and unpacking the brownies. Joe sat, languid, in the chair, staring at the rug.

"What's wrong?"

"Nothing."

"You're jealous."

"Yeah."

"You're not me."

He snorted.

"Look Joe, I'm not going to let you bring me down. I'm sorry you're pissed, but I'm not going to let you bring me down." (I was getting strident.) "When I try to cheer you up, you get mad at me. You have to be coddled." (And why not? What's so wrong about that?) "I don't know what you want."

"I'm tired of being alone all the time," he said.

He said it so simply, so without affectation, I was stung. I said something to the effect that I understood, but it was a throwaway. Then I said fast, "Let's go lie down."

He followed me into the bedroom listlessly. We lay down on the bed together. I took him in my arms and kissed him on the neck. He kissed my neck. We were quiet for a while.

"Why don't I give you a massage?" I asked. "I don't think we have everything worked out between us, but we can do that. Maybe you'll feel better. And we don't have to do anything else if we don't feel like it." Sounding like Nurse Greer Garson, but softly.

So I massaged him without oil, then he massaged me a bit, and it was different, quite good. He's something of a mind reader by now—he unbuttoned my jeans as I hoped he would and rubbed my belly.

"I like that," I said. "I'm very—uh—responsive tonight." We laughed.

Lying together a bit later, I asked him if I could lick his ass. He stiffened. "I'm not going to rim you," I said, half joking. "I just feel like licking your ass."

He allowed as how the idea didn't especially turn him on, but he let me do it. Since I'd been massaging his ass through his jeans while he lay on top of me and he'd been pretty hot over that, as he usually is, I figured he'd like a little ass work. He loves to have his ass pushed and pulled when I massage him.

So we took off our jeans and shorts. He lay face down on the bed, and I licked up and down his legs, then lay down between them and licked and bit and kissed his ass—which was really quite picturesque in the light from the bedside lamp, that ass, every mole and hair of which I know so well. How anyone could lick that ass and not dive into the crack to the asshole is quite beyond me. But I resisted.

I turned him over and began to blow him. He hardened up in my mouth, then we traded off a while. Then I went—as they say in the porno magazines—"crazy on his cock."

And he came! Hurrah!

He jerked it out of my mouth, laughed, and shivered up and down the length of his body.

He blew me for a while then. But I was pretty enervated by this time and just generally glad for Joe, not so interested in it. So I jacked myself off. And though I wondered for a while there if I'd make it, I did.

*

Sammy said, "People can only go as high as you go yourself." And, sticking a finger up my ass, "People can only get as hot as *you're* hot."

Tonight I was eating dinner and watching TV. A story about a pediatrician. The kindly doctor was filmed on his rounds.

All day long at work something had been flickering about the edges of my consciousness, something dreamed perhaps, perhaps something someone said....

The doctor cut through a child's ribs on the operating table. I began to cry. I managed to swallow the food in my mouth. I put the napkin over my eyes and cried....

I grew up in a small Western city where one of the summer attractions was a musical comedy performed in the city park and sponsored by one of the newspapers. From age eleven until well into high school I acted and sang in those shows. We kids cavorted and mugged around the stage while the Wells Fargo Wagon was a comin' down the street or everyone was declaring in four-part harmony what a real nice clambake it had been.

The year I was thirteen, I began riding to and from rehearsals with a schoolteacher who lived a ways out of the city, in one of its eastern suburbs. Taking the bus all the way downtown alone and then back home in the dark was an ordeal. It was much more fun riding with Ted.

He was a popular amateur actor who usually played comic parts in our summer shows and, during the winter, appeared in little-theater productions. Everyone loved him. He was a card. I liked him because he was funny and intense. He looked as if he'd stepped directly out of *The Inspector General*: long, string-bean body, Adam's apple like a fist, prematurely balding.

Driving home one night, Ted brought up the subject of hypnotism. Casually.

"Ever been hypnotized?" His eyes alit on me briefly, then returned to the street.

I said I hadn't. He said nothing more. Shifted gears. Silence.

Why? I asked.

"It's just . . . kind of a hobby with me."

Again, shifting gears, busy concentration on the traffic, street signs—like a man miming driving a car.

I asked him about it the next evening, of course. Did he think *I* could be hypnotized? What made some people easier to hypnotize than others? Are you unconscious, in a trance?

He smiled indulgently at my questions (keeper of the mysteries), answered with a patient air, and saved his proposal for the next night.

"Would you like to?"

Be hypnotized?

"Yeah."

I didn't know. It might be fun, I said.

"I don't hypnotize just anyone. I think I'd only put you in a light trance"—as if deciding—"to begin with."

And so he did.

That night and the following night—and the next night, after rehearsal in the marble pavilion in the park. He drove to the other end of the park, next to the reflecting pool, behind a stand of pine trees.

I have no doubt that he put me in a real trance and that it was impossible for me to move my arm, that the pinprick in the back of my hand (the pin drawn from under the collar of his jacket) didn't hurt, that his hot breath in my hair, as he put his arm around me to raise my right hand above my head and leave it dangling there, thrilled and frightened me almost inexpressibly.

One afternoon on the way to rehearsal, Ted parked the car under a red maple (like the two trees in our front yard at home) and hypnotized me. He had me rub my face in his crotch, over his dark brown serge trousers. Then he opened his fly and had me rub my face in his underwear. I remember the smell.

That night he had me do other, painful things.

I asked him not to make me do them. "You won't do anything you don't really want to do," he said in his hypnotist's voice.

I knew that was true and that I had wanted him to do something I wasn't quite sure of, in the beginning. I knew who, what, I was; what I wanted. Vaguely.

I ate my early dinner alone in the kitchen. My mind was fixed on the jockey shorts I'd washed in the toilet the night before, now deep in the bottom of the hamper.

It was almost five. Time for Ted to pull up in front of our house, honk his horn, open the door for me. Time for the wisecracks, the commentary on current events, the bony hand reaching over to squeeze my knee. Time for rehearsal.

I went into the living room. I put on my sweater. I looked out the front window. Too late now to retrieve the jockey shorts. Too late to take them out to the trash. I waited at the window.

My father came into the living room, rummaged through the desk.

The car pulled up in front of the house.

I said good night to my father.

"This guy Ted," said my father. "Is he all right?"

I stood at the screen door, looking out at the car. Ted honked, once.

"Oh, sure," I said to my father. "He's a nice guy."

"You're sure."

"I have to go."

And I slipped out the door. . . .

Tonight, with the napkin over my face, remembering what I'd so desperately and successfully forgotten for twenty years, I realized why I don't trust men.

⚑

Not dead yet. My father at seventy, dying of cancer. But not dead yet. The cancer is spreading through him like dye through water, but he's not dead yet.

I no longer await his death impatiently, to get it over with—as if he would die and I could dust off my hands, walk briskly away from the grave, and be rid of him at last. But it's easier for me to think of him dead than it is to force myself to realize that he is alive, thousands of miles away, but dying; that he will die painfully, not long from now, far away.

Tonight I held the pillow and beat it as if it were my father. But finally I set the pillow aside. I lay in the middle of the bed. The tears and snot dried on my face.

⚑

"He knew."

"_____"

"He knew something. How could he ask, then ask again, and not *do* something?"

"_____"

"How could he?"

"_____"

"He knew and he didn't do anything. But I didn't want him to know, did I?"

"_____"

"How could he let that happen to me?"

"_____"

"That night I hid the underwear under my mattress. I put it in the incinerator and burned it with the trash the next day. My mother asked me what happened to my shorts."

"_____"

"I see a child on the street and I want to protect him."

"Yes."

"I see myself in him."

"_____"

"I loved acting."

"Yes."

"And I didn't let them ruin it for me. I didn't let them stop me."

"_____"

"How could he let that happen?"

"_____"

"I didn't want him to know. I wanted him to tell me I didn't have to go with Ted."

"Yes."

"I beat my pillow, pretending it was him. But it's too late, isn't it?"

"_____"

"I feel sorry for that boy."

"Yes."

"_____"

"Danny, what are you feeling now?"

"I'd like to find that man, that Ted, and kill him."

"Yes."

"Because he was like me, and he did that to me."

"Yes."

"I feel sorry for that little boy."

"_____"

"I would like to help that little boy."

&

Not dead yet. And now I want to hold him, talk to him, help him through this death. I remember the terrified eyes. I want to wipe the terror from those eyes.

&

"What *is* it you think you wanted?" asked my composer friend.

✦

Middle-aged, married, with children—a man began to write me. Long letters, describing his lovely house, his study, his books, his solitude.

Of course you were right, he wrote. *There's nothing for us. I'm grateful for that one night.*

Two, three letters a day.

And if you should call, I don't care if you call me here at home. I can't believe I'm writing this, but I don't care. You can call me here.

Letters written by hand, late at night.

I completely understand how the phone calls irritate you, he wrote. *But I have no one else to talk to about this.*

In the evening, in the morning, phone calls at my office.

"What are you doing right now?"

Until I stopped answering the phone.

I was glad to get your letter. I know you can't keep up with mine. And you aren't being cruel. I'm being cruel, but I have to write you. It is four a.m. I can't sleep. It's not you.

Until I stopped writing.

I would like my letters back, he wrote. *And I will perhaps give them back to you, because they are for you, after all. But I would like to read them. Nothing like this has ever happened to me.*

I saw him again in New York.

Why did you go to the hotel with me? he wrote afterward. *It was not, as you said, to prove we could be friends, that you could be there with me. I don't want sex from you. I don't want that between us again. But why did you go to the hotel with me? I can't help but think that it was some kind of revenge. And that it has nothing to do with me. This gives me some, an abstract kind of comfort. That it had nothing to do with me.*

Then the letters ended.

✦

Revenge.

✶

Not dead yet. I sat in the bedroom, the last day of that visit, dressed in my suit and black tie, bags packed and waiting in the hall. I held my father's hand.

After a while, he took his hand away, on the pretext of scratching his temple. There were three framed photographs on the wall over the bureau—my sister, my brother-in-law, me. The photographs were studio portraits taken long ago. On the bureau, there was an old photograph of my nephew, a blond child on a swing, in an easel frame that had once contained mine. The shades were drawn, but the windows were open and the room was cool.

My father cleared his throat.

"They say," he said, "that on this medication, you lose your sex."

What would that be? To lose your sex? Even at seventy? When it is a bond between you and her? That thing enduring?

"Perhaps—not," I said.

He didn't answer.

"We want you to live," I said.

"Yes."

So they can drain you, cut you away piece by piece. Is that why?

The room was silent again. No reason to repeat that I loved him. No reason to repeat that I was really just a few hours away. No reason to wait for an answer I wouldn't receive.

In the kitchen my mother was talking to the cat.

In the easel frame, the little blond boy seemed to dip on the swing, coil his legs, pump the swing into the air, perilously high above the clipped hedge, the picket fence, the sidewalk beneath him. . . .

✶

"What was he like?"

"He was very quiet. Nice. Well-liked. Everyone liked him. My friends liked him."

"What did he look like?"

"He was very—boyish. He seemed very naive. I felt very—paternal toward him. He seemed lost. He wasn't lost at all. *I* was the one who was lost."

▲

Sitting in the living room tonight, I watched Joe through the bathroom door. Combing his hair. The part. The points behind his ears. Preoccupied.

Joe is not my lover. We're moving apart. I can't protect him. He'll be himself without me.

I am in the dark television room at the Club Baths, watching an episode of *Centennial* (remembering stories my cowboy grandfather told), and two men are fucking, virtually at my feet. When I came in, they were napping, but during one of the commercials they woke up and started feeling each other up under the blanket, which was soon tossed aside. Now one is lying between the legs of the other and fucking the daylights out of him.

My little towel is tented up in front of me. This is the first really erotic thing that has happened to me this evening. I've decided I'm not really a baths person: even on assignment from Virgil, I can't get it on here. Maybe the place is too clean, too California, with its potted palms and pink downlighting. Maybe whatever has blocked my responses in the past is especially strong here. Maybe I'm scared—of what?

Certainly when Joe and I came here last week I was hysterical with apprehension, babbling like a Baptist Youth let loose in a Times Square arcade. Certainly the tables had been turned and were spinning like a merry-go-round, as Joe (who had never been to the baths before) led me up and down stairs, held my hand in the orgy room, plunged me into the Jacuzzi to calm me down.

Joe *loved* it, couldn't get enough. Right now he is upstairs in our room/web with a fabric designer from New Jersey. They've been up there over an hour. I walked by a few minutes ago and the moans coming through the door and over the partition indicated they were having nothing less than a hot time. The grin on the face of the man hanging over the wall from the next booth and watching them set a seal on it.

This is amazing, considering what happened to Joe earlier this evening. We had fulfilled our assignment last week by practicing blowing each other in our room here. The idea tonight was to "bring other people into it"—another step in our transference to tricking. Joe stepped out of the room with me after we'd manhandled each other a bit, and directly into the arms of—yes, a troll. When Joe met up with him later on, the guy was so insistent that Joe freaked out. He thought he might as well "get it over with." So Joe let the troll steer him into his room, where he was promptly raped. I met up with him on the stairs just afterward. His hair was full of Vaseline, and his eyes were wild.

I took Joe back to our room and lay on top of him a while until he settled down. I was worried. But I needn't have been. Five minutes later Joe was on the prowl again. Ten minutes after that I found him at the coffee machines, deep in conversation with the cute blond from New Jersey, who, after various complications and arrangements, managed to get Joe up to our room. Joe: ever the blushing virgin.

The guys at my feet cum and lie back down on the carpeted floor, pulling the blanket back over them. My attention has been rather divided—between the big shootout on the screen, rustlers versus good guys, and the big shootout not four feet away from me.

I've been through the labyrinth, in and out of the orgy room (one lonely figure hunched over on the floor in the darkness), sat in the sauna (one lonely figure, me, sweating out his assignment), made several fruitless tours of the halls, the poolroom, the stairs and cribs ... for nothing. Hands politely removing mine from thighs and chests. Hands not so politely waving me out of doorways. Hands reaching out for me in the dark corridors, hands attached to bodies that to me held all the appeal of corpses pickled in formaldehyde.

You see?

No wonder I'm having a rotten time. In this Howard Johnson's of the heart, this supercharged Boys' Club, this clean, well-lighted place, I can't get the Everard Baths fire and those nine dead men out of my head. I keep looking for the exit signs; sure enough, they are everywhere. It's neither death nor sentiment that dogs me down these carpeted passageways, though. It's the secret of sexuality that everyone here but me seems to possess, even the "trolls"— who know what they want and how to get it. Even the trolls can smell me yards off. My panic. *Them* it turns on. Everyone else it turns off.

No, Danny boy, this is not the place for you. Maybe some other time. Maybe never. You bring in a stink with you.

Afterward, Joe and I go to Phebe's, an East Village hangout, for a hamburger. Joe has the fabric designer's phone number in his pocket. For my sake, I think, since the tables are still spinning, he says he's not sure he'll call the guy. He doesn't quite know how to take his success, what to do about me, even though I'm perfectly happy now and asking him for all the details—happy just to be out of the Club Baths, happy for him. Yet he is diffident about telling all. I remember, in the shower that time, how he fantasized me into Tony Perkins, butcher knife in hand.

But jealousy's not what's bothering me. You see, just three days ago *I* held the secret to sex in my own hands, just as Joe holds it now after being worked over so lovingly and competently by the designer—to an extent that he almost forgot to jack himself off once the guy had cum doing the Princeton rub with him. ("Do you mind?" Joe asked him. "It's real important for me to cum.")

What's bothering me is that I have the power in my hands now to set the tables careening wildly in a counter-clockwise direction with the velocity of a turntable floor in a fun house.

I cheated on Joe the other night.

᛭

"You were so wild. So unhinged. I don't know—so *sexual*," my political friend said. "What were you on?"

He'd called me up for dinner the day after the party.

"We didn't know how to take you. You were—there's no other way to put it—hostile. All those cracks about whether we should dance to the Village People because they were exploiting us, and then dancing with that woman and taking half your clothes off and dry-humping her in the middle of the floor like that. What were you *on*?"

"I was having fun," I said weakly.

"Well, we were really worried about you. What's happening to you?"

His hadn't been the first call that day. Everyone was "worried" about me, it seems, and the Jekyll-Hyde number I'd done at the party.

Something snapped, I guess.

So this Oriental woman, Beatrice, and I went off to the Cockring and continued to dance our buns off. Then, when she left, I saw this cute guy boogying alone and asked him to dance. And we did, and it got more and more sexual, our shirts off, fingers hooked into each other's belts, thighs thrust between each other's legs . . . until I steered him off the floor and down the corridor to the back hallway and we were all over each other. From there it was just a few painless steps out the door, down those enchanted few streets to my apartment, into my shower.

And real sex. Shower, shared biographies, a cup of tea,

pulling back the sheets, and—like a swift, sure Latin declension returning in a rush of memory years after the last class has been let out—real sex. Of a distinctly adolescent kind, perhaps, but real sex nevertheless, with all its noises and other paraphernalia.

I jacked myself off. ("Do you mind? It's real important for me to cum.")

Did I think of Joe? Once? Sure. I put him out of my mind. After the Flamingo fiasco with Gatsby, I wasn't about to queer this one.

I cracked up in bed the next morning (actually, two in the afternoon) with the schoolteacher snuggled beside me.

"Yeah?" Beguiling Brooklynese burr in his sleepy voice.

"It just hit me." I hesitated. Why not? "I'm in sex therapy."

"Could have fooled me."

"Yeah?" Flattered. "Anyway. I just cheated on my partner."

⚑

Like the rat I was, I made an appointment with Virgil the day after Joe and I went to the baths. Virgil reminded me that the agreement not to have sex with other people was with *him*, not with Joe. Chagrined, I nevertheless plowed ahead and laid out my worry that Joe would be mad, jealous, would flip out over the fact that I'd tricked. And, worst of all, that I had had a great time again, just as I did with Sammy.

"You'll have to tell him," Virgil said.

"Yeah," I said.

"I imagine he'll be angrier over your coming to me first than the fact that you did it."

⚑

The next night, Joe told Virgil all about our night at the

baths, the rapist, the fabric designer from New Jersey, what a bummer the evening was for Danny, how great it was for him. I sat back and let him tell it. He shot me a few apprehensive looks as he did so, asked me with his eyes to confirm this or that point, rattled on as he seldom had before—and I thought what a transformation we were seeing in Joe, from the silent, scared kid he'd been the first few months, wringing his hands and desperately longing for Virgil to put all his misery into words for him. . . .

I thought of the fantasy he'd had a few weeks before, when he'd forgotten we were meeting an hour later than usual and had rung Virgil's bell, got no response, and waited in the foyer for Virgil to come home or come downstairs, let him in. He imagined being stabbed on the street by a mugger, dragging himself to Virgil's doorstep, ringing, ringing. . . .

As if somehow Virgil had the power to "save" him.

Not now.

My vertigo intensified during Joe's recital. I felt like throwing up. Virgil's eyes were locked with mine. The room was silent. Joe had finished.

"You want me to say something now." Not a question.

Joe's face had confusion, fear stamped on it.

A

We were silent in the car on the way downtown. Then, when we got into the apartment:

"My fucking heart stopped! I didn't know *what* you were going to say! You just left me hanging there. Christ! I didn't know *what* to think. That you were dropping out. That you found a lover. That you got fist-fucked by fifty men at the Mineshaft. Jesus! Why didn't you tell me? You didn't even apologize. You went to Virgil! What'd you two plot together? What a rat you are."

A new Joe. And I refused to apologize. That, I refused to do. Not just because I wasn't going to apologize for the sex, which was good. But because I was simply a rat.

For once, he refused to listen to reason. For once, he refused to have it analyzed. For once, he didn't succumb. He was murderously mad. Then he slumped into a silence more murderous than his words.

He knew me well enough to know the prime weapon. If you don't talk to Danny, it kills him.

⚑

Well, *that* was a lovers' quarrel, I told myself. Obviously, he was obsessed with the fact that he didn't own me. I'd been *unfaithful*. Well, he *didn't* own me. *He* wasn't going to hold me back. I'd shown I cared about him, cooling my heels and my ass downstairs in the fucking TV room at the fucking baths while he fucked for an hour and a half upstairs. I was all charity and understanding, didn't desert him there, the fucker, and the New Jersey guy had a friend, too. . . .

But he was right. Even though he didn't give me a chance to explain. Even though he gave me the silent treatment. Refused to fight it out. He was right. I was a rat. I didn't trust him enough to think that he could have dealt with it on his own. . . .

The next time we saw each other I made him fight it out. But it was too late.

⚑

Joe is not my lover. We are moving apart.

⚑

I am coming home in the evening and turn the corner onto my street when I see The Man Who Walks His Dog. Back to me, he is in the middle of the block. Even though his dog is squatting out of sight between two cars and his back is to me, I would know The Man Who Walks His Dog anywhere—just by those buns.

I slow my pace. I don't want to be next to him when he

picks up the dog shit with the sheet of newspaper in his hand—which he does, and walks to the trash can, drops it in. The terrier is scratching at the pavement with its hind legs, like a cat.

I am carrying a bag full of groceries. Nothing frozen.

The dog stops to pee.

"Hi," I say to The Man Who Walks His Dog.

"Hi," he says, recognizing me and giving a little jerk on the dog's leash to get it out of my way.

"How about this weather?" I say, not exactly falling in step beside him but not in a hurry either.

"Isn't it something?" he says.

It is either unseasonably warm or cool. It doesn't matter.

"You live up the block, don't you?" he asks, pointing.

"Yeah," I say, giving my street number. "You? I see you out a lot."

He lives on this block.

"Would you like to have a cup of coffee sometime?" I ask.

"Sure," he says. "I have the dog. . . ."

"Yeah," I say.

We look down at the dog.

"But if you don't have any frozen food in there," he says.

"No. . . ."

"Why don't you come up for a cup now?"

Just neighbors chatting on the street. Old friends who haven't seen each other in a while.

I follow those delicious buns up the stairs. The dog, let off its leash in the foyer, capers up ahead of us, nails clicking on the linoleum treads.

On the very top floor of the house, he takes out his keys (on a chain tucked into his back pocket, very butch) and unlocks the door. He steps back to let me enter. As I walk into the apartment, his hand briefly touches my waist.

The dog goes into the kitchen and laps water from a pan. It glances at me, then goes on drinking.

The Man Who Walks His Dog closes the door behind us. "I lied," he says. He is leaning against the door.

"Lied?"

"I don't drink coffee. Have a seat."

I put my groceries down. "I have a quart of milk in here," I say.

"But nothing frozen."

"No. *I* told the truth."

Smiling, he bends down and takes the milk out of the shopping bag. I allow my fingers to rest on his back. He gives my knee a little tap, then walks into the kitchen to put the milk in the refrigerator.

"I *do* drink tea," he says from the kitchen. "Unless you'd like a drink."

"Tea's fine. I don't drink coffee either." I walk a few paces around the living room. I hear water running into the kettle.

"Nice place," I say.

It is either comfortable or dreary. It doesn't matter.

"Thanks," he says. He comes to the kitchen doorway and looks into the living room.

"Lot of plants," I say, pointing to the windows.

They're either healthy or starved. It doesn't matter.

"Have a seat," he says again.

I sit on the couch. He leans against the doorjamb. He smiles again.

"Have you lived here long?"

"Lived around here long?"

"Yeah," he says.

"Not really," I say.

Now his hands are at either side of my head, resting on the back of the couch. His face swims before mine. He smiles again. The kettle is whistling on the stove. He kisses me. I let my hands rest on his hips.

"We used to have a whistling teapot at home," I say. "I always lose the top to mine."

"Yeah," he says, and stands up.

I put my foot between his legs, raise my shoe until the

toe nestles into the crack of his ass, nudge his crotch with my ankle. He leans back against my foot.

"I lied," he says.

"Lied?"

"I don't really like tea either."

"No stimulants?"

"I don't need them."

. . . .

The dog licks my bare foot. The sun has gone down. The room is dark.

The Man Who Walks His Dog is softly snoring at my side. I still have an erection, just from the heat of his body.

I have either cum or not cum. It doesn't matter.

⚑

"Whatever happened to gentleness?" I ask my feminist friend. "Whatever happened to dating? Whatever happened to meeting people at dinner parties?"

"That's what *I'd* like to know," she says.

⚑

I know that soon we have to go out and trick. Virgil hasn't said when. I don't know what he's waiting for. But I dread the time when he tells us to.

I will have to go out and trick. But not the same way, and not on the same circuit, up and down Christopher Street to the dockstrip and back.

One thing that Virgil has emphasized is my drinking. A certain kind of person, he says, likes to pick up people who are drunk—the kind of person who has often picked me up in the past, when Friday and Saturday nights were synonymous with alcohol for me. The kind of take-charge man to whom I gave myself over so easily and whom I loathe. And in a way, having those encounters at four in the morning, depressed and passive from booze, did more than ensure my failure: it also mitigated my failure by excusing it.

And we know now, don't we, who that take-charge man really is: yet another variation on the Hypnotist. The Good Father, who loves and protects, has for so long been in a tug of war with the Bad Father, who abuses and betrays. And both of them are warring inside of *me*.

⧗

The other night I complained to Virgil that I didn't fantasize. Everyone fantasizes, he replied. Yes, I know that, I said. But mine are like dreams for someone who never is able to remember them. What's going on inside me now? What is that rich imaginative life I know we all have? What isn't reaching the outside?

Virgil reminded me—The Man Who Walks His Dog.

"But The Man Who Walks His Dog is a real person," I objected.

"Is he? How do you know?"

"I see him all the time."

"But you've never talked to him."

We decided that it's a good sign that I'm able to fantasize about someone again.

To be sure, Max and many of the others I was in love with were walking fantasies of my own, not complete people, and often people upon whose features were superimposed those of the Hypnotist, the Father, others. Virgil once said in our group that this is typical of a certain stage in relationships, and the seed of their demise. "People will insist on being themselves," he said. "They don't conform to the initial fantasy."

As long as Max and I could be in love in a certain way that was not touched by certain realities, sex was good. Ironic, because I was always so careful in bed with Max not to fantasize outright. Joe and I are (were) both ashamed of fantasizing (when we did) with someone else.

When I was in bed with Max, my fantasies were quite rigidly suppressed. And one of my greatest insecurities was that Max was fantasizing all the time. But now I'm hard pressed to say which would have been more real, my fantasy of Max as my constant and faithful lover, or whoever I might have fantasized Max into as he was fucking me.

⚼

Joe is blowing me. I lie back and close my eyes. I'm trying to fantasize without the aid of the porno we (I feel) rely on. Nothing happens. I pick up my magazine. I'm able to forget it's Joe doing those things to me. It's better. Not enough, but better.

You know, I can't remember the last time I turned out the lights and lay in bed jacking off, using only my imagination. And—like not using the dildo or any of the number of things Joe is willing to do to help himself—I am resistant to fantasizing solo. It makes me sorrowful to think of jacking off alone. Not because it's a solitary act. It is, after all, the only sexual pleasure I was able to have for two or more years. But because I can't seem to relate my fantasies to real life.

But that's why they're fantasies, you'll tell me. Yes. And yet I prefer the company of Captain O'Malley, working over the Corporal (me) in the barracks. I prefer that to fucking the stable boy in the midst of the Victorian fantasy I'm sometimes able to conjure up, in full color, directed by Joseph Losey. Why is it safer for me to use other people's fantasies than to have my own?

⚼

Do I really want to be tied up and beaten, as I fear poor Max wanted to be? For real? Max had that done to him. Once he almost didn't walk away from it. I didn't exactly satisfy *his* needs either. . . .

⚼

Thinking how in many ways Max and I were a perfectly

matched pair of S&M lovers—except for the fact that we didn't do S&M in bed. I know now it would have been more healthy there.

⚑

Max wasn't so different from the rest of my lovers—I *chose* all of them, after all—but in one important way he was. For two years, day and night, I went through a growing regimen of denial. As effectively, then, as if I'd consciously signed up for a tour of duty, I put myself in Max's hands for a course in desexualization. *How* this happened is probably banal and boring to the extreme—"pure Dory Previn"—but I'm appalled all over again at what Max and I did to each other.

⚑

The images in my porno magazines: "Maybe they're pragmatic," says my political friend, "but ultimately they're dull and dehumanizing." How many of them are increasingly, at least peripherally and often dead-center, S&M?
I've never done S&M. Is that where this is leading me? Away from my pale pastel English country house and into the dungeon below the dark castle on the hill? What kind of man will I meet there? What kind of man will I be?

⚑

Captain O'Malley unlocks my shackles and allows me to stretch my arms, my legs. Then he takes me up in his arms and places me on the soft sheets. Slowly and gently, he bathes my wounds, the welts across my back, my torn asshole, the rope burns. He turns me over and applies a cool salve to my aching nipples, my bruised cock. He kisses me on the forehead and stares into my eyes, from which the tears still stream. I have bitten a hole in my lip. I did not cry out (but once, in submission) through the long ordeal.

He stares into my eyes. He is proud of me. He loves me. Turning out the overhead light, he leaves me to sleep in the cool darkness.

Was it the beating or the aftermath I craved more?

△

I was talking, talking, talking in circles.

Virgil stopped me. "Pick an object in the room," he said. "Pretend that you're that object. Talk as if you *were* it."

This is easy, I thought, after all the acting classes I've had.

A little spotlight attached to the wall (used for Virgil's videotape sessions) caught my eye. "I'm that spotlight," I said.

"What do you say?"

I closed my eyes a moment.

I am a followspot in a huge theatre. I am trained on the stage. The auditorium is empty, the curtain raised, the stage bare, but I am focused on the stage. My spot is searching the stage, into every corner, onto the apron. Looking for something to light.

"Interesting," he said when I'd finished. "Interesting that you were only as important as the actor you had to light. Let's do it again."

I closed my eyes.

No. I can't do that.

"What do you see?"

No, I can't.

"Do you see anything?"

My eyes are closed.

I am in a tall tower. A wooden ladder leads up to the tower. The tower sits at the junction of two high barbed wire fences. The fences stretch off into the distance. There are towers like mine, regularly spaced along the fences.

I am a spotlight. I am the color of a revolver. I am hard, cold, blue metal. . . .

"What do you see?"

I can't.

I am—raking—a wide expanse—a huge yard—a pen—frozen mud. . . .

"What is it?"

I am cold. I am hard. I am raking the yard with my cold blue light.

Barracks. The glass broken out of the windows. It is night. The barracks are dark. They huddle inside, against each other. For warmth. They are plotting. Plotting their escape. . . .

"Who are they?"

But they cannot escape. To venture one step outside the barracks is to enter my cold light. To be frozen in my hard blue light. . . .

"What are they doing?"

They huddle together in the frozen barracks, lips too frozen to curse. My hard blue light rakes the yard. . . .

"Who were they?" Virgil asked, when I opened my eyes.

My eyes were full of tears. I unclenched my fists.

"Jews," I whispered, shaking now, trying to hold back the tears. "But they were also, they were also, they were gay. Trapped by my light."

⚑

A photograph in my copy of *Drummer*: a punk sitting against the wall of a shed. He wears black leather chaps, nothing under them. His tattooed chest is bare. A motorcycle cap sits on the back of his head. His face is unshaven, a sneer on his lips. In one hand he holds his hard cock. With the other hand he gives you the finger. On one of his biceps there is a swastika.

⚑

Leather men call initiation into S&M "a second coming-out."

▲

Max lay beneath me, eyes shining, mouth agape. I could see back to his tonsils.

His legs were braced over my thighs. His toes dug into the sheets. He slowly worked his cock. Intermittently, he would gasp or moan, but always he urged me on.

His stomach muscles clenched and unclenched. His thighs trembled and twitched. The ring of his asshole quivered.

"Go on," he grunted. "Go on."

Four fingers slipped in. Then I eased them out to the rim and slid in my thumb. I urged my hand in, up to the knuckles. His asshole expanded like an iris. He gave another grunt.

"Your cock now."

With the cool precision of a practiced student of anatomy, a scientist, no more—I leaned in, placed my cock in the palm of my hand, rocked my hips forward.

The skin was tight over his skull. He expelled a sigh through his open mouth. His body was covered with sweat.

My mind was not attending to the motions of my body. My mind was floating above Max, whom I loved at this moment more than I had ever loved. I tried to fathom the black eyes.

▲

"We've found you have a sadistic streak," Virgil said.

"And a masochistic streak, too," I said. "Which am I?"

"Do you have to choose?"

At long last! The green light.
Our latest assignment: find someone you *really like* and trick with him.

("But darling," says my novelist friend. "That's just what we *all* want!")

♠

I hesitate. My finger is poised over the telephone dial. The number stares up at me from my address book. I have left Saturday night open. I have planned for this. This is what I've been waiting for for two months. I remember his chest in the *V* of his unbuttoned shirt. I remember his slightly hooded, slightly reddened and sexy eyes, brown eyes with long lashes, underscored with mauve shadows. His smile, slightly awry. His touch on the back of my hand as we sat at the bar, having a drink. The tacit question in his eyes.

Then we walked out into the street. It was painful and irritating how shy we both were. It was excruciating to be trapped in that shyness and to know the only way out was by talking bullshit. But there was a fit of sorts; he felt right. And there was an attraction. All right: lust.

I told him I couldn't have sex with anyone right now, but that I'd like to have sex with him when I could.

"I don't know what he thought," I told my Fire Island friend.

"I do," he said. " 'Another fucked-up queen.' "

⚑

The idea, of course, was to get him into the shower, heh-heh. And right on cue, it began to rain when we left Clyde's. We bought the Sunday *Times*, and I held Sports over my head. He steadfastly refused to take Real Estate. We slogged on down Waverly in the cold rain. Every once in a while we bumped up against each other.

It had been a dreary cabaret-coffee-and-cake evening. The only thing that saved us was our mutual malice toward the performers.

This was, I was sure, no way to start. But here we were.

I *really* liked him. But it had been such a long time coming, so to speak.

I showered, but he wouldn't come in with me. Then, as I was getting us a drink, he went in and showered himself. When he came out, I was on the bed, reading Arts and Leisure. He picked up the Book Review and sat down beside me, dripping wet, inches/miles away.

It won't work, I thought to myself, turning pages. It's too important to work.

Then, as if by previous agreement, we set aside the paper and lay down together. He slipped into my arms. Every time he moved above me on the bed, cold drops of water fell off his curls onto my face and shoulders. "Warm you up," I said.

He was cool. Working at me almost frantically, hard as granite. But cool. Not *with* me, nor I with him.

The categories marched through my head: Mutual J.O. Sixty-nine. Rimming. Tit-sucking. Body rub. Foot-tonguing. Frenching. Face-fucking. A greasy finger up the ass. Lick the armpit. Ball sucked into the mouth. Stroke thigh. Grab ass. Chest to chest. Friction. Blow in the ear. Suck. Squeeze. Wrestle. Heave. Shove. Buck. The ceiling. Music on the stereo. Cock straining up.

I sat on him. We smiled. He arched his back. Slow. He put his hands behind his head. Drove in slowly. Ha. The last thing I thought I'd be doing tonight. His face, dim, distant, as if through a peephole lens—let me in!

I jacked myself off.

When I came out of the bathroom, he was reading the paper again.

⚑

"So they left and I was standing next to the dance floor, sort of moving with the music, when I saw *him* again with his friends, and he looked over at me and winked. Winked! I was *so* embarrassed. Then this girl came up and asked me to dance, she was very stoned, and I said sure and we started dancing—and she's *coming on* to me, kissing me and putting her arms around me, and I'm pushing her away very gently. So we get off the dance floor after a couple of dances, and she's *all over* me. And I say, 'Look, maybe you don't understand.'—even though this *is* a gay bar, for godsake—'I'm gay.' '*I* know that,' she says. 'Just go with it.' I push her away again. 'But you don't understand,' I say. 'You're ruining my image.'

"So I go into the bathroom and comb my hair. *Very* embarrassed now. And I go back out and there *he* is (and I hope he didn't see me with the girl) and I go right up to him...."

"Thank God," I say. "Finally."

"Yeah, well, I go up to him and say, 'Wanna dance?' Then I immediately begin to walk away...."

"Of course."

"He just looks at me. 'Wait,' he said. 'Sure.' So we dance. Danny, he was *so cute*. My height, dark like me, Italian, real blow-dry, with this John Travolta body shirt, but *so cute*. And we're dancing. Then it's last call and he says, 'Wanna go home with me?' And I, ah, say, 'I don't know.' So he says, 'Wanna have a cup of coffee? We can have a cup of coffee.' So I say, 'Okay.' We go out into the parking lot and I say, 'I'm not sure I can come home with you,' thinking that I didn't know whether I *really* liked him or not, and he says, 'Look, we don't have to do anything. Let's just have a cup of coffee.' So we go to this diner and have a cup of coffee—he's this decorator, why do I always get the decorators?—and he says, 'I really dig you, Joe. I really do.' "

"So what happened?"

"So I was still wavering. Not knowing. He was really cute. *And* intelligent. Anyway, he says then, 'Why don't you come over to this place this friend of mine lets me use sometimes and we'll, like, have something to eat or something and we don't have to do anything?' I was *so* embarrassed. This cute guy. So we went, and it's this fuck place. . . ."

"Fuck place?"

"This fuck pad this guy, a straight guy he knows, this guy has to bring his mistress or whatever. What a setup! It's kind of sleazy. You know. Nice sleazy. With all this crushed velvet modular seating, but with lots of plants hanging around, at the windows and from the ceiling, above this garage. . . ."

"Like a garage attached to a house?"

"No. This is near my town. I pass it all the time. A garbage-truck garage. It's this Mafia place. I know this friend of his is like Mafia. Garbage. Anyway, it's this huge apartment with a sauna, a Jacuzzi—"

"A Jacuzzi?!!!"

"Yeah. Isn't that too fucking much? A Jacuzzi. A little one. And all this *bad art* on the walls. He's very nice. And a kitchen with a microwave oven and stuff. No bed. I don't know where the bed was. Maybe in a wall or something. So he puts out these big pillows and we sit down and have a glass of wine—I'm thinking I'd better have a drink to relax—and we talk and then he says, 'Wanna use the Jacuzzi?'

And we get into the Jacuzzi and I feel very relaxed, we start to kiss. . . ."

Oh, Joe. My man Joe.

"Real sexy like. Kissing. So we do it. Until four in the morning. Finally, I jack myself off—it was easy—and we go to sleep. . . .

"Then, when we get up the next morning—ah, Jesus, it must have been about eleven, it was light out when we fell asleep—he's wearing these drawstring pants. Oh, Danny, he was so cute. But he was real distant. Like he didn't want me to touch him. He was friendly. He made coffee and everything. But distant. So finally I got the hint and said, 'I better go.' 'Okay,' he said, not very enthusiastic, and I left and we said we'd see each other around. What do you think about that?"

"Are you bullshitting about the Jacuzzi?"

⚠

I doubt if I've ever been so highly motivated to do anything (unless it was to fail my draft physical) as I am to go out and trick. But having Virgil finally say it's okay has had an interesting effect on me. I can't keep my hands off myself. I am not only jacking off with my porno before I go to sleep at night, I'm also jacking off in the mornings and sometimes between the evening news and the Carol Burnett reruns. I've had periods like this before.

But I think that, instead of keeping myself in a state of sexual preparedness for that chance encounter that will win me an A+ in class, with all this jacking off I'm actually resisting with all my might the idea of tricking at all.

I've also developed a slight tic. Very attractive. It manifests itself in potentially sexual situations. My actor friend noted it when we were walking down Christopher Street the other day.

"What's that?"

"What?" I thought maybe I'd been careless with my napkin at lunch. I wiped my mustache.

"No. That," he said, still pointing at my face.

A young Latino with a silver stud in his ear was peering into the window of the Leather Man.

"There. You did it again."

My hand went back up to my face.

"That twitch. Your face is twitching."

"*Dark Victory*," I said automatically. "The one where Bette Davis falls down the stairs."

He followed my gaze to the kid's buns. Then he smirked his most condescending smirk. "It's okay, Danny," he said. "You're allowed now."

"But would I *really like* him?"

My cherished celibacy is backfiring on me in unanticipated ways. It has, on the one hand, retrained me not to keep my eyes firmly planted on the ground when I reach the vicinity of Sheridan Square (or Seventy-second Street and Broadway, or Forty-fifth Street in the theater district, or Fifty-third Street and Third Avenue where the hustlers are, or Bloomingdale's, or. . . .). On the other hand, having been temporarily restrained from committing myself sexually, and therefore being *somewhat* relaxed, I have gotten used to actually *looking* at people.

Now, looking is not the same thing as cruising. It's a kind of way of touching base, especially outside our dear ghetto, amidst straight folk. Comforting to lock eyes with someone and acknowledge that you're not alone in alien territory. *I've gotten used to looking.* I even *enjoy* looking now.

That hyperconsciousness of our difference that gay people have—it has a dark side that can approach paranoia. All those years in the closet—under the imperative of not slipping, not being found out—make their mark on you. I used to have two modes only: not looking and cruising. I often confused the two. Once we had "cruising lessons" in my therapy group, when one of us maintained he didn't know how to. But how reluctant we were to display our expertise! We practiced on each other, did a little role-playing. "You might look at him," Virgil suggested to me, "instead of standing there like a statue."

How many bars have I stood in like a statue? Dozens. How many hours on how many weekend nights? Thousands. I *have* learned now to look and theoretically I might learn to unbend. But I fear (I know) that when thus transformed I get back into the bars, there will be lots of Old Dannys there—not looking, hoping that someone will approach them just because they know that deep down inside they are neat guys.

A

I feel like the boy in the glass bubble, the one who was born without defenses against ordinary germs. The spirit is willing, even tuned into human contact. Inside I'm every bit as horny as my Fire Island friend ever aspired to be—which is pretty horny. But these old habits surround me, protect me from the contact I still fear like the plague.

A

"But Danny," says my novelist friend. "You were always a cocktail-party pickup. Cocktails at the very least. Peking duck if possible, with all the trimmings. And even then, without the hansom cab ride in the park, almost impossible to land."

"I have never ridden in a hansom cab in my life," I say testily.

"Or the equivalent," he says airily. "How did that gypsy from *Follies* land you? He took you to Provincetown."

(It's true. And I had the time of my life cooking little dinners for the two of us on a hotplate in our little cabin.)

"But Danny," says my political friend. "One of the most refreshing things about you was always your focus on the inner person. You're a highly socialized person."

"I used to go to the trucks," I say loftily.

"If I remember correctly, you were thrown out of the trucks."

(It's true. I was singing "We Kiss in a Shadow." Softly, but I *was* singing it.)

"But Danny," says my Fire Island friend. "You're not even aware of what you're doing. Remember that guy I introduced you to at the Metropolitan? At the Avedon opening? You talked to him for hours. And nothing. Then you tell me on the way downtown you would have blown him on the grand staircase for a dime. Who knew?"

"Even *you* thought he was too pushy," I say like Grumpy.

(But it's true. My sexual desires always gallop away from me and into the fog, like wild horses, and I'm left standing in the stable with a currying brush in hand, making passes at thin air.)

"What are you waiting for? An engraved invitation?" a man said to me on line at the Superette the other day. And I became aware that I'd been staring at his basket—not his shopping basket.

I'm not ready!

I almost left without my change.

⚐

I did it.

Just back from San Francisco, where he'd moved "forever" to get away from New York, my carpenter friend called me up the other day and we met for a beer at Fanelli's in SoHo, my friend's favorite bar. It's a Depression-era holdover—and holdout from the waves of high-tech chic that threaten to engulf it: signed prizefighter glossies, cracked and mottled, hang on the walls; a magnificent, much-varnished gingerbread bar; a cozy back room.

We sat in the back room, the two of us and a motley collection of artists, neighborhood people. Of all the aging hippies there, my carpenter friend was the only one who didn't look either depressingly malnourished or somewhat obese. I reflected on the incidental benefits of being gay.

Would we, too, be potbellied in our early thirties, unkempt, sallow as these people, if we hadn't come out?

My friend's hair was surprisingly short and it was the first time in years I'd been able to see his entire face. What had happened to his beard and flowing tresses?

"I went to San Francisco thinking I'd fit in," he sighed. "But everyone out there's been cloned"—referring to the Castro Street look—"to such a degree that I stuck out like a sore thumb. I'd even dug out some old love beads from my Flower Child phase, but I never got to wear them. I cut off my hair. But it was very depressing out there all the same. Most of the time, walking around, I felt as if I'd been plunked down on Parris Island. Thank God for Lennie. He convinced me to come back."

"Lennie?"

He took a sip of his two-bit beer. "Lennie. My new loftmate. You've never met Lennie."

"No."

"Sweet guy. You'd like him. . . ."

We went up to my friend's loft, which was unchanged in its squalor from the last time I'd seen it. Evidently the sublet, to the dyke photographer ("Susan Wimmenkin" she called herself), hadn't worked out. My friend wired Lennie his distress from San Francisco. Just in time. Lennie was looking for a place to share.

When we got there, Lennie had one arm in a bucket of plaster. I shook his free hand. My friend went back to the hotplate to fix a pot of tea. Lennie hurled himself at a sheet of Masonite. Arm first. Most of the plaster and a fuzzy impression of his arm and hand remained on the Masonite.

I didn't ask him what it represented.

While Lennie scrubbed up, we drank tea and further deplored San Francisco. Then my friend excused himself to go out and buy dinner. They urged me to stay on.

("What have I missed?" my friend had said earlier. But I didn't tell him about my sex therapy, perhaps because I want to get used to my gradually-blossoming new identity as someone who can "function.")

Lennie's cornflower-blue eyes peeped out at me over his cup of tea. I admired the way his thighs filled out his jeans, his hunky wrists, his capable-looking hands.

My friend called up to say he'd been waylaid by a customer (was this true?) and that he had to make a call downtown, would be back in an hour. He hoped.

Lennie brought out a big jug of cheap red wine.

I stood in the W.C., swaying over the toilet, bracing myself with a hand against the wall—not because I was drunk but because ever since my carpenter friend had left I had been so tense that I felt weak.

When I came out, Lennie was stretched out on the studio couch. He'd kicked off his shoes.

"This is a person with whom you might have a relationship," said the unbidden voice of Molly Goldberg.

He was fiddling with a blond curl at his temple.

"Why don't you lie down here?" he said.

"He has a B.A. in Ecology from a fine Eastern school," Molly reminded me. "You are the same age as he and share many common interests. Furthermore, he has a promising future, according to your friend—would he lie?—in the field of his choice, as an artist. But he is sensible enough to pursue an ancillary career as a laboratory technician at one of our most prestigious metropolitan hospitals." She shook her wooden spoon at me. "He is a mature man. A *mensch*. And he is not encumbered by other emotional commitments. *That* he has made clear."

"But, Molly, if I do it I'll have to see him again. And what if *he* really likes me? But, Molly, he's very dullll," I whined.

"Do what you please," she said, turning her back and stirring a pot of something fragrant and nutritious on the stove. "Is it *my* life? If you lived in Sioux Falls, South Dakota, my young friend, you'd gobble this nice boy up."

"But, Molly, I'm not *ready*."

Lennie patted the Indian print spread.

A

"Mainly I just lay in his big strong arms," I told Virgil and Joe. "He was slow and gentle. He said he loved blowing me. He said he loved the shape of my cock." (A glance at the well-endowed, uninterested Joe.) "He was a great kisser."

"Did you cum?"

"I sat on top of him," I said, remembering the feel of Lennie's furry thighs against my bottom. "And I jerked myself off. He took it in his mouth. But this is so. . . ."

"What?"

"Clinical. He was a nice guy."

"Are you going to see him again?" Joe asked.

(Surely I was imagining it, but was he vaguely threatened?)

I looked at Virgil's bookcase. For some reason, surveying the books in Virgil's bookcase was a more pressing task than answering Joe's question. Finally I said, "It would mean a commitment, I think. And he's so"—shamefaced, casting my eyes to the floor—"dull."

"Is that all?" Virgil asked.

"No. I'm sure it isn't," I said. "I'm just not ready."

"And how was *your* week?" Virgil asked Joe.

Christmas already. Joe gave me a tie—"not from Korvettes." I gave Joe my novelist friend's new book, even though Joe says he never reads.

"But it's a gay novel," I said.

He looked at it rather skeptically.

"Pretty cover," he said.

But the next day he called me at the office and said he'd read it in one sitting, the night before.

"Jesus," I said, astounded at his speed.

"You did say it was—what did you say?—a thin volume?"

"Yeah, but really."

"I've never read any novel written for us."

⋏

My mother is very excited. I'm flying to San Jose. This will be the first time we've all been together as a family in fourteen years. It's kind of a command performance; we're all nervous about my father. His cancer has been "in remission" for a year and a half now, but lately he's been having a lot of new aches and pains. I have secret conversations with their doctor, long distance. He once told me that when it happens it will happen fast—the next step, the final step we all dread so, is chemotherapy.

My parents are thoroughly adept at denial. The doctor says he tells them as much as they ask for. And I know they're both acutely aware of what's actually going on. But they act as if they aren't. I don't know, after those phone calls to them on Sunday afternoons, who's protecting whom. I suspect my mother (who is the strength and motor of the family) is protecting my father from any articulation of the truth. Of course the word "cancer" is never mentioned. The word "death" never even enters the conversation.

My mother is very excited. They will fly to San Jose themselves a day ahead of me. The three of us are going to my sister's. My parents sent me money for the ticket, and my mother has requested "token presents" from me. Needless to say, I won't bring "token presents." For one thing, my sister and I have not exchanged real presents all these fourteen years.

How can this be possible? I love my sister dearly. She's much older than I, but I rediscovered her when I grew up and was no longer the brat who flushed her bobby socks down the toilet. Perhaps our family rather exemplifies the Western ethos: keeping on the move over enormous distances, not placing much emphasis on ties or history, making the world over in our own individual images. It is no mistake, for instance, that my sister ended up in California. She is a very California person—one of the conservative stripe. However the reality of her nomadic life might contradict old-fashioned values—"You're the kind of person," she once said to me during the Sixties, "who destroys property"—she adheres to them and then some. I love her and, as I said, I appreciate her, but necessarily from a distance.

It is no mistake, either, that *I* ended up in the East, as if deliberately seeking out some place as unlike the West of my childhood as possible, having alighted in several temporary stations along the way until I finally settled in New York.

New York: it terrified and elated me. So thoroughly alien, so other. So different from the open spaces of my upbringing. So different. Like me. I came out in New York.

And then came out to my family. I did it aggressively and badly. My political friend and I went over several drafts of The Letter together. And I rubbed their noses in it. How much residual self-hatred there was in my "politically correct" action! For I wanted them to see what they had done to me, what I really was. . . .

But I also wanted to be close to them. I sincerely wanted them to know me, Danny. I wanted to fill the void secrecy had created between us. What had always been a blank spot—my emotional life—had grown into a chasm. I filled it in.

My parents barely spoke to me for two years.

So much for politically correct action. It had the desired liberating effect, forced me to make a life for myself without them, never easy for Good Boys like Danny. But what else was new? I'd been doing that right under their noses and in their own house most of my life. Is that a condition of being gay?

My mother is very excited, but I know she's also quite terrified—that I'll want to talk about *it*, my homosexuality. She has gradually learned how to defend herself, though, through a technique my actor friend calls her "And Then I Told Doris" routine.

My parents visited a couple of years ago, and my actor friend and his lover had them up for dinner. "So they should meet a really bourgeois faggot couple," my actor friend said. It seemed like a good idea.

My father was ICE, of course. My mother complimented them on their decorating.

"Why, thank you," said my actor friend. "We've only been here for a year and we really haven't had the time or money to—"

"And then I told Doris," said my mother to me (*I* was downright comatose that evening), picking up on an obscure monologue from that afternoon. . . .

Doris, Mary Elizabeth, That Nice Man Down The Street—it doesn't matter who. Each of them serves to knit tighter the net my terrified mother throws around all potential discussions of *it*—gay life, my life in New York, me.

Whenever my actor friend and I laugh about "And Then I Told Doris," my friend's lover says, "I think it was actually very *brave* of them to come that night."

And he's right, I suppose. "We can't think about *it*," my mother once said to me, in a rare moment of candor, and out of a clear blue sky. "We could dwell on *that* if we wanted to. But I'm not to blame"—she's right—"and I've learned to hold my head up high"—in the face, I'm sure, of a lot of heavy questioning from the neighbors and the ladies at church.

Ah, well, her obsession with *it* is only second to mine. And I'm certainly capable of accepting the inevitable: that I will slowly melt away during these five—five!—days away from home, at home. That I will return to New York reduced, as is typical, I suppose, to age ten—and worse, a eunuch.

My therapy group has instructed me to "talk to" my father.

▲

Ecstatic about being back in New York. San Jose was pure limbo. Flew in over Manhattan, over the Empire State Building, Brooklyn—all etched out white and stark under a clear blue winter sky. Surprisingly, no one was in when I made phone calls, not even those lucky devils who ate my Fire Island friend's legendary Christmas goose (paté stuffed prune stuffing) in exile from Grandma's house.

Sat next to the window with the phone on my knee, looking out onto the street, exhausted, glad to be home.

Conversation in San Jose mainly limited to: 1) Mother's stories about us as kids; 2) Football on TV—to which I contributed some butch comments; 3) The peanut brittle I brought all the way from New York, a big hit and always a favorite of my father's.

I was not asked what I'd been doing.

"Oh, I have this guy who comes in regular twice a week and we suck each other's cocks, but it's all right, it's part of this sex therapy we're doing, you see. . . ." I did not say that at any point.

The second day I was there, we saw the sights of downtown San Jose. The six of us (my nephew is a giant, at sixteen) stumbled around awhile until we came upon a little greasy-spoon restaurant. We were all very hungry (*I* was looking for a Taco Bell, something uncontroversial), and my mother read the menu in the window of the restaurant none of us but her would think of considering. We loitered on the sidewalk while she read us each item. "I bet we can get a real good hamburger here," she said. She used to run a hotel dining room and has lots of theories on where you can get the best this or that.

(That hotel dining room. . . . You see, she'd won a scholarship to a little Nebraska college, but her father refused to let her go: they'd installed a smoking room for women. She has never, since then, stopped striving, stopped trying to learn, stopped trying to have new experiences.)

We went in. It was a miserable, flyblown place, but, as my mother pointed out, the tables were clean and the kitchen was open to the rest of the room. It passed muster, too.

None of the rest of us was talking by then. It's an infection that courses through our family, like the Black Death. It begins, of course, with my father, who barely talks at all unless baited or otherwise incited—and then usually it's a few clipped sentences. My brother-in-law is a replica of my father—not exactly Milton Berle. My nephew, being sixteen, has nothing to say to the likes of us. My sister talks very little around my mother. Although they are, as she says, finally friends—well, the competition between two high-powered women is pretty keen. My sister prefers not to compete.

My mother, of course, when faced with this wall of silence (*I* long ago stopped conspiring with her against the two of *them*), becomes almost hysterically garrulous.

She fiddles with the condiment stand on the table. "That relish looks fresh," she says, oblivious to the hippie waitress behind the counter, who, since the restaurant is virtually empty but for us, can hear quite clearly what is (or isn't) being said at the table.

We're seated around a table for ten. It's the only table that would hold us, but the symbolism is excruciatingly painful for anyone with an eye for it: chairs separate us as my mother tries to make a unit of us.

"Look, honey," she says to my father, "it says here the fries are Idaho potatoes. You love good fries. And, Tom," she says to my brother-in-law, "they have fish sandwiches." (Tom must like fish.) "I think I might have a Sloppy Joe, myself. Remember how you used to love Sloppy Joes, Danny?" ("Um," I mutter.) "But that turkey breast sounds good, too, doesn't it? Except we're going to have turkey tomorrow," nodding in my sister's direction, acknowledging her once-a-year stab at real cooking.

Now, be fair, Danny, be fair. These five people (including you) aren't being so cruel to this poor woman as it seems. It can't be that bad.

But it is just precisely that bad. Eating, when the food finally comes, is a relief from the shameful spectacle of our utter silence. We cram it in with gusto. We keep our mouths full. All of us but my mother, of course, who is pretending we've come to a nice hotel like the one she was forced to work in and are having a nice, leisurely lunch.

How like life, as my novelist friend would say, surveying this scene. How like every vacation the Slocums ever took in utter silence to Mesa Verde or Salt Lake City. . . .

But wait. What is this I hear? It's my mother's voice in the front seat of the old Studebaker. She's singing. It is late at night in—Nebraska? Kansas? My mother is singing a Depression-era ditty. Cheerful, reassuring. But what is that I hear now? It's my father's voice. He's singing now too.

Darkest Nebraska, a hot muggy Nebraska summer night, oppressive as only those August nights in eastern Nebraska can be. Heat lightning flickers over the rims of the hills. Thunder rolls toward us. My sister and I are curled up in the back seat, our legs sunburned from having been stuck out the open windows all afternoon. My father and mother are singing. The voice on the tape and its mate.

In whose life?

In the motor court, my parents slept in a big iron-framed bed painted to resemble oak. My sister and I slept in trundle beds like big drawers that pulled out of the wall. My sister and I were frightened of the thunder and the big show the lightning was putting on outdoors. My mother was thrilled, for she was back home in Nebraska, and what had frightened her before, when she was a child, was a sweet reminiscence now....

"Little boys love their mothers, little girls love their fathers," I recall my sister saying.

Oh, no, no. I remember that night vividly, as I lay in that drawer-bed on the kapok mattress, already thinking at that young age (six, seven?) what I thought my father would expect me to think: that they, these females, were silly creatures; that *he* was not frightened of the lightning, so I wouldn't be either; that *he* was beyond such painful sensitivities. Purely sentient of one being in the cabin, overwhelmed by it as I was by the awful thunder of that Nebraska night, I lay watching my father in the darkness while my mother tried to soothe us and herself with a dream of a Nebraska night that never might have existed but in her wishes....

In whose life?

Oh, no. I watched my mother, too, with an eagle eye. I felt her every joy and every pain as if it were my own. I type-cast myself as her with Max (another stony type, like my father). I adored her, admired her. But did I love her as I loved my father? Never. Not in a million years. His was the love, you see, most precious—because withheld. Hers was abundant, ubiquitous, easy. You just kept your nose clean and she loved you, no matter what. She still loves you,

Danny, in spite of *it*. In fact, if she had her way, she would probably learn to *understand it*, if not accept. . . .

But no, it's him. This little drama is revolving around him.

"This is just delicious brisket," my mother says to the waitress. "So lean."

"Thanks," says the waitress, warming to the compliment. And by the time we push back our many chairs and edge our way to the counter to pay the bill, my mother and the hippie waitress are chatting away like fast friends. She's put the old whammy on her, just as she does to people on buses, in elevators, at the supermarket. It is a trait of hers, endearing really, which I never emulated, needless to say.

Out on the sidewalk, she pulls me over to a shop window, taking my arm and pointing out some turquoise jewelry—"Just like that necklace you bought me in Arizona, remember? When you were just a little boy?"—and in the reflection on the window I can see my father watching me from the curb.

It is hard to describe the expression on that face. Dispassionate, you'd say, but faintly curious. He is definitely looking at *me*—my mother has sidled off to the next window—as I pretend to peer at the jewelry, while the other three saunter down the street in *their* tight little family unit.

Who knows what he's thinking.

I remember what my actor friend once said about that nightmare evening at his house: "Danny, your father is always looking at you. He loves you so much. He's always looking at you when he doesn't think you'll notice. It's as if he's almost *cruising* you. You fascinate him." I dubbed this nonsense, and even now it disconcerts me to see the evidence of it reflected in the shop window. Especially now. . . .

He turns away and looks up the street, as if searching for some *deus ex machina*, perhaps a skyhook or a UFO, to take him away from here, San Jose, us, his utter isolation. Or am I projecting? No, I've seen that stance before, a million times. And the eyes narrowing, the angst spreading across his features, the evidence of emotion—unaware of its existence perhaps—and evidence of thought unconfirmed by human contact.

"This is it," my mother says, pointing into the window. "It's just like the one your father bought me two Christmases ago." A jade ring set round with tiny diamonds. "I forgot to bring it with me. It's really a cocktail ring. You know. Or did I show it to you when you were home?"

"No, I don't believe so," I say.

"I didn't? It's really a cocktail ring. I wear it out to dinner. I can't believe I didn't show you that ring."

"I don't think you did."

"It was the loveliest present...." A vague reference— or is she even thinking that as she admires the ring in the window, *her* ring—to the Christmas of the fire-engine red nightgown, the Christmas of the lacy baby-doll pajamas, to all the Christmases of fantasy gifts duly exchanged for something sensible.

My father has joined the others, halfway down the block. My mother takes my arm again and we stroll toward them. But she stops at any shop window that catches her eye or fancy in dreary downtown San Jose. She is stubborn. She will have her pleasure—or pretend to.

"I like that color," she says to me, running her fingers down my shirt sleeve. "It brings out your eyes."

"Thank you," I say.

My Fire Island friend gave it to me for Christmas. My novelist friend gave me a very fancy fountain pen—though he knows I don't use one—the same kind he uses to write his novels. My actor friend gave me a Venetian leather wallet— though he knows I don't carry one. My political friend gave me a copy of *Gay American History*, which I have promised to read in full. My feminist friend gave me scented soap and a beautiful back brush because she says people should have luxury in their lives. My composer friend gave me a tape of his opera, *Blood Wedding*, which was performed only once. My dancing friend gave me his promise to take me to the Sleaze Ball in the spring.

"Thank you," I say to my mother.

▲

My sister gave me a plastic paperweight with a picture of a frog embedded in it and the caption "i like you just the way you are." It was in my stocking (treasured from childhood, brought with me from New York) when I got up Christmas morning.

Though she likes me the way I am, she will not tell her son what that is. He's "not old enough yet," she says. And besides, she wants me to get to know him.

She doesn't have to tell him, I'm sure. He is curious about his Uncle Danny, but edgy. At one point on Christmas Day he emerged from his room long enough for me to shanghai him into driving me out to see his high school.

"Why do you want to see an old high school?" he said.

But he took me. He's very proud of his car. He rebuilt it inside and out. It's a powerful machine. He's a nice kid.

We talked about The Meaning of Life.

▲

On my last day there, I took my father for a walk around the block, the only way I could get to talk to him as per instructions. We were like two Gary Cooper clones walking through Death Valley. Near the end of our walk, I finally said, "You know how much I love you?"

"Yes," my father said.

Who knew what he was thinking?

Long silence. We walked up the driveway and leaned against my brother-in-law's Buick.

"I spent a long time running away from home," I began, not knowing what I was aiming at, feeling needy and apologetic. "I thought I had . . .something . . .with Max."

"I'll never understand that," my father said tartly.

I knew he didn't mean Max but my homosexuality. "Oh," I said (the light touch), "we were immature. He didn't know what he wanted. Thought he did. Love wasn't the question."

Home.

But I guessed then that he was setting Max and me alongside his love for my mother, and I was not measuring up; so I asked how she was doing during his illness. He said they didn't talk about it as it upset her too much.

And I learned who was protecting whom.

I changed the subject, but he wouldn't play. After a while, he said, "Let's go inside." He began limping to the front door. Our walk had gotten to his leg. "Leg hurts sometimes," he said. I followed him into the house.

✪

My sister was putting towels into the dryer, out in the garage. I went out and closed the door behind me.

"I tried to talk to him," I said. I was very upset. "But I can't."

She didn't look up. Just kept packing the towels into the dryer.

"You both should have talked a long time ago," she said.

She was angry at both of us—but it was also my only peek behind that cool façade she presented all those five days, at her anxiety that all go well, that her father die with at least this, this Christmas.

✪

At the airport, as we were saying goodbye, I hugged my father. When we pulled apart a bit, I could see his throat working. He was choked up. He turned away, much as he had turned away from the little boy with the blistered lips. A woman was watching us with a big smile on her face, as if we were a living Norman Rockwell cover of father and son—which we were, I guess.

It's not the last time, I was saying in my head. I'll be there at the end. I loved him, but it was his ball game now.

⚕

And as we were sitting down in San Jose to our Butterball turkey Christmas Day, Joe's family on Long Island was finishing their espresso. The dining room table was littered with dribbles of sauce and bread crumbs, bits of green salad. Joe's sister from California was there with her kids and her contractor husband. Joe's other sister, from Union City, was there with *her* kids and her junior college teacher husband. Joe's mother and father were there, of course, and Joe. The kids were playing in the living room.

The two brothers-in-law were arguing about California. Can-you-top-this? Income. Lifestyle. "All the freaks in the country," said the junior college brother-in-law. "Bozos, cultists, queers. I wouldn't raise kids in that state." The contractor brother-in-law talked about Proposition 6, the one that would have banned gay teachers. "I voted against it," he said, "because even if you *weren't* queer and just talked about it, you could lose your job. They could fire *anyone* on that. It was too broad."

Joe just looked down at his coffee.

They agreed that queers are sick. Studies have shown that they are sick. It isn't normal.

Joe went into the living room. He sat down on the couch. They were still talking about queers in the dining room. The kids were playing with their new toys. He didn't feel mad, just sick to his stomach.

"I know this guy who I go into the City to see twice a week and we have sex together. But he isn't my lover. It's complicated. What do you think of that?"

This New Year's Eve my Fire Island friend, my dancing friend and I had several parties to go to. True to form, we didn't make them all, but we hit quite a few. Our novelist friend stayed at home: "Just me, a bottle of gin and *Vile Bodies*." His latest ("A nice sadist, and what a welcome change of pace from the little masochist I was going with—you have to cater so to their *every* whim. . . ."), his latest was still visiting his parents in New Orleans.

When did New Year's become a strictly gay affair for me? It must have been the year after my feminist friend's big blowout up on Morningside Heights. My actor friend, his lover and I were the only gays at that enormous, legendary party—legendary for the amount of misbehavior that went on between the sexes. Legendary as well because for the first time since my playground days I almost got into a fistfight. I was dancing with my black friend and when the Stones' "Brown Sugar"—doubtless pirated into the party by some low-consciousness type—came on the stereo, we went over and took it off. I convinced her not to throw the record out the window, but she was quite vocal about the fact that *she* wasn't "brown sugar," and that's when several Harvard boys attempted to put the record back on and there was a set-to between us and them, followed by a strategic retreat on our part, though we were still in possession of the offending LP.

That, however, was long before the Harvard boys started stripping off their tuxedo jackets and boiled shirts, screaming for pussy; long before the author of *Shrike: A Feminist Manifesto* attempted to mutilate her male lover (a sometime saxophone player and an illegal alien) with a broken champagne bottle; long before an editor of *Grass-roots* magazine threw up all over my feminist friend, ruining the silk blouse she'd just brought back from China; long before the piano was wheeled out into the hall and sent crashing down the stairs—*"Take the music to the people!"*

But long before those legendary events, we three gays left, agreeing in hushed tones that straight people were hopelessly uptight.

▲

This New Year's, somewhere between the third and fourth party, 1979 began. It might have been around the time we got off the uptown local and on the crosstown shuttle under Times Square. Our dancing friend capered down the passageway ahead of us, in thrall to his characteristic hyperkinesis. My Fire Island friend and I wove our way in and out of the crowd, trying to keep up with him. Everyone was pressing to get out of the subway into Times Square before the ball descended, ringing in the new year.

New Year's most probably took place on the shuttle to Grand Central, very quietly. We were the only people in the subway car. Our dancing friend was spinning around a pole, like a kid let out to play.

We made a monster party uptown in the East Seventies. The five-thousand-dollar sound system, blaring a disco tape specially created for the evening, went to waste; no one was dancing or talking or eating. Two hundred or so beautifully dressed men milled about, each of them evidently under the impression that he was Romanoff nobility brought low, into inferior surroundings. One hundred of them seemed to be drinking Perrier with a twist.

My dancing friend couldn't bear to see all that amperage squandered. My Fire Island friend (on a coke buzz) was neutral. And I was—reflex reaction—looking around for a rich husband.

So we went downtown. A few more parties, then we ended up at our cartoonist friend's loft on Spring Street. Our political friend was there, and our carpenter friend, and Beatrice, the woman I so shamelessly dry-humped last November.

"This is more like it," I said to my Fire Island friend.

Our dancing friend was boogying with our political friend, teaching him some new steps.

I was determined to have sex, a New Year's present to me from me.

"Want some punch?" I asked my Fire Island friend. But he wasn't listening. He'd spotted his Summer Romance across the room.

The guy hadn't changed one whit since the Island; he was still as tall and tan and young and lovely as he had been last August. I figured that there'd been a winter Caribbean cruise—that tan—with his dentist lover.

My friend's eyes were without expression.

How did the affair end? Well? Badly? He's never said. He's almost pathologically reticent about such things. So I should speculate? Well, it *was* a summer romance, just that.

I pulled him out into the center of the floor to dance. But the Summer Romance, wherever we danced in that huge loft, seemed to crop up right beside us with his dentist lover in tow. The four of us danced together, parted, met up again. And my friend was utterly *subterranean*.

If it hadn't been for my therapy, I found myself thinking, would *I* have been his summer romance? Silly, perverse question to ask, well into winter, well into a durable friendship blessedly unfettered by the obligations and ambiguities of love.

Just because you flamed out over Max, don't think others are so—volatile.

I put my finger through one of his belt loops. He grasped my arm, and we spun around together. His eyes were *not* on his Summer Romance, but my normally overactive imagination was still running amok. I wanted to step on the Summer Romance's feet, trip him up, or make him disappear. How dare he pretend nothing happened last summer? How dare he smile and try to be just plain friends? How dare he shake his firm, round buns under my friend's nose?

Later I saw the Summer Romance and his lover go out the door. Off to another party, doubtless, or Flamingo, then to bed, perhaps with a third, a Romance-for-the-Night, a plaything, another assured noninvolvement. How cozy to have such a lover as the dentist, to be tall and tan and young and lovely and a perfectly wonderful person, to be so adept at noninvolvements and still to be able to have a Primary Other. . . .

So you did so well yourself, Danny? Jealous?

Why was I getting so worked up?

We took a break. Our dancing friend and our political friend had proceeded from the bump to the rock to heavy body dancing. The few straight couples in the room were doing a modified bop. Our carpenter friend was in the corner French-kissing his loftmate, Lennie.

"How're you doing?" I asked my friend.

"Fine. A little tired."

"They left."

"Who?"

"Your summer romance and his dentist."

"Oh."

"You're looking just adorable tonight," I said.

"Thanks. You drunk?"

"No. Not particularly."

"I think I'll go home," he said.

"I was thinking of going down to the Cockring or something."

"Walk with me, then."

We walked up West Broadway. It was about three in the morning and I was feeling great. We walked across town. At Sheridan Square a boy lay on the sidewalk in the rain, next to the subway entrance, passed out, his coat folded under his head for a pillow. Couples in fancy dress were looking for cabs. A lone transvestite was picking through a garbage basket, found a pizza crust, ate it.

We stopped at the corner of Hudson and Christopher.

"Have a good time," my Fire Island friend said.

"I'm not sure I'll go now," I said. "The walk's sort of done me in."

"Well," he said.

"Wanna just curl up together and sleep?" I asked.

"Naw," he said, then looked at me sideways. "What do you mean?"

"Just what I said." (But did I?)

"I don't know what that is," he said slowly. "But it makes me nervous."

"Okay," I said. "Just a thought."

He looked away a moment, then back to me, then smiled. "Good night," he said.

We embraced and he walked away, up Hudson.

I looked down Christopher, toward the docks.

Why was I blurring everything with sex? Feeling sorry for him? Feeling sorry for myself?

"What is *it you think you wanted?"*

A full-bodied love with all the continuity and intimacy and depth of friendship. Impossible?

So don't fuck up your friendships over it, Danny, I said to myself. They'll be around after the next Max, and the next.

And don't reflect too much on the extent to which your friends—as did your lovers—have become aspects of yourself.

What did I do? I went down to the Cockring and picked up this guy who I wasn't really interested in at all, and I took him home and, finally, lying beside him as he slept, I was able to cum.

▲

Joe drove slowly past the garbage-truck garage. There was a light on upstairs. He recognized the guy's car and one other with Jersey plates. He had a slip of paper with his phone number on it in the glove compartment. He'd had it there since the week they tricked. But he didn't stop.

▲

The other night, Virgil put forth this new theory that we might jump ahead from blowing if we start fucking, and that then we'll be able to blow.

So he gave us (for him) very detailed instructions about fucking. Shower together and get comfortable. Then investigate each other's asshole. "People know what an asshole or a cunt *feels* like," he said, "but they don't usually know what one *looks* like. Get to know your assholes." Joe has no trouble with that, of course.

We're game, but just barely. We follow his instructions to a tee. Parting asscheeks as if putting our fingers into a basket we secretly think is full of snakes, we peer at each other's asshole. Pandora had nothing on us, peering under the lid of her box. Gingerly we finger each other's asshole. Silently we reposition. Work fingers into each other. Fight off the impulse to giggle. Grease up. Start wisecracking. Sober up.

Joe lies underneath me. I caress his chest, nipples, his stomach. I sit up and spread his legs. Stick in one finger. He is limp. Caress his cock and balls. Two fingers. He gets hard.

"Want me to?"

He nods.

I am very hard. Easily distracted, but very hard.

"How?" he half whispers.

"Maybe if we—spoon-fashion. It might be easier the first time." First time, I think. You must be joking.

We lie on our sides, me behind him, stroking my cock up and down between his legs, into his crack. He is pumping his not-quite-hard cock. I am still very hard. Put my fingers in again, press my cock against them, as if I could get cock and fingers in at once, clearing a path for it, so to speak. I slip my fingers out and press my cock against his asshole. He is moving against me.

I go limp.

"Huh."

"Huh?"

"I—ah—I lost my hardon." Still pressing, as if it would go in. More rubbing. Stroking. "Can't."

He turns over on his back. "Huh."

I clear my throat.

"Why don't you let *me* try, then," he says, with a trace of condescension, just a trace.

"All right," I say. There is an edge to my voice. A dare.

He tries. I lie on my stomach and he strokes himself until he's hard. Then he leans into me—and nothing.

He lies down beside me. "I guess we don't want to do this," he says.

"I *guess*." I laugh.

We lie there, smirking at each other.

"Wanna blow?" he asks. So we do and he cums. I can't get it on at all. "We do enough fucking, I'm going to be impotent," I say. I have to return to the barracks with Captain O'Malley to get off at all.

𝄞

So we go back to blowing. But there's no escaping the fact that we're tired of each other and a pall is falling over the grand experiment. Not even the news that Virgil plans to write us up in a psychological journal perks us up. He obviously considers us to be great successes, and we *have* come so far. . . . But we are terribly dispirited. Each of us secretly believes that we will be jacking ourselves off with every trick we meet from now on, that there are some things so complicated and ingrown that not even Virgil can help.

Part of it is that we're tired of each other. Our attempt

at fucking was an acid test of sorts. Self-defeating, of course, but how can you fuck someone you don't feel you can even kiss? Oh, I know you're supposed to be able to and that countless men do in tea rooms and at the baths. But that isn't us. We can't just vault from sisterhood/buddyhood to lust with a snap of the fingers. Not Joe and I. With other people? Maybe.

Keep at it, Virgil says. He's distressed that we've been taking little vacations from each other, skipping sessions. We promise to keep at it, but *it* has become formless. We're ready to quit, though neither of us has said it.

▲

Every man for himself, now that we're supposed to trick. Tricking. Every man departs alone into that great maw. You go out to dinner with a friend, then stop off at a bar for a nightcap. And each of you knows the evening is really over, the nice time you had together, when you enter through those doors. You have a drink together, cruising the room surreptitiously or openly as the case may be, and then one of you goes to the john and (perhaps) disappears without so much as a good night.

▲

The other night Joe and I experimented—in the chair, on the floor, different positions—but I couldn't cum. As a matter of fact, my *hardon* came and went. Very depressing. Finally I came (on the bed), jacking myself off, a very sleepy Joe yawning discreetly beside me. He drove back home at midnight.

We discussed it with Virgil tonight. His first question was "Why are you withdrawing?" And I realized I had been, emotionally. It seems Joe and I can only get so much mileage out of each other.

Joe was edgy. "Withdrawing?" Was I making a unilateral move out?

"What have you been thinking about lately?" Virgil asked.

The answer, of course, was Max. Max, who appears and reappears in these pages—sometimes in the traditional black garb and bristling mustache appropriate to a villain, sometimes surrounded by a white aura and gowned in innocent unassailability—like an unsuspecting ghost called up from his slumbers by an officious rap on the table. Who is Max today, or what? I suppose he's more of a phantom than ever, certainly more than ever a creature of my dreams, and the phantom holds some kind of torch in his hand, a light illuminating the future, when I'll allow myself to love someone again.

I apologized to Joe, who seemed to understand.

☀

Big party the other night for my novelist friend. He is about to go off "on tour" to promote his new book. He has given us all a printed itinerary and enjoined us to send him "all the dish, as I will be leading a completely monastic life in little hotel rooms."

It was some party. His designer friend sent out telegrams as invitations. "This is so impromptu," he told us at the door, "that we completely forgot about the food." In fact, he'd sent out for Chinese—deluxe, from the Shun Lee Palace. (My political friend was all but totting up the bill on his fingers.) They emptied the braised eggplant, the sweet and sour shrimp, the ginger beef into beautiful one-of-a-kind lacquered bowls, put them on the table with mother-of-pearl inlaid chopsticks, and served it all on Limoges. Very impromptu.

"Aren't you glad you turned out gay?" my dancing friend said *sotto voce* to his new boyfriend (guess who?) in the living room. "How ever would we have met such people?" My political friend blanched a bit.

Someone circulated through the room after dinner with "party favors"—LSD wrapped in little foil squares.

There was dancing and general merriment, and everybody got pretty wasted. I didn't take my party favor, but I did get drunk. I had a long conversation with my doctor friend about Hepatitis B and the new vaccine they're developing. Then someone broke his foot doing the stomp. . . .

I was standing outside the john at one point with another guy and, what with one thing and another, we fell into some innocent sex play. When the bathroom door opened, we slipped inside together and started smooching. I worked his sweater and shirt up over his chest, revealing what might possibly have been the most beautiful tits in New York. Our glasses were fogging up.

I tried to piss, but couldn't. He stood behind me, playing his cock back and forth between my legs and across my ass. My trousers were down around my ankles. I turned around, put the toilet seat down, and blew him a while. By this time people were knocking on the door—spoilsports—and we went out, separated, melted into the crowd.

Later on my novelist friend introduced him to me. "How d'ya do?" we both said.

For some reason, a man wearing a leather harness, reputed by my novelist friend to be an eminent psychiatrist, had gotten it into his head that I'd earlier proposed having an orgy with him and his lover. He kept coming back to me and reporting on his recruiting efforts.

My bathroom buddy kept in touch, too. Every once in a while he would come up behind me and put a hand down the back of my pants.

"That man who was feeling you up," said my novelist friend, "might possibly have the most beautiful tits in New York."

"Really," I said.

"We have to stop meeting this way," said the man with the tits later, outside the bathroom.

We took a cab to my apartment.

In bed I told him he had what might possibly be the most beautiful tits in New York. He flexed them for me. We tussled a little bit. I was hard, but he wasn't. He went down on me. I sucked his tits for a while.

"I bet everyone wants to do this," I said between mouthfuls.

"Yes," he said. "Feel free, though."

"It doesn't—uh—seem to be turning you on."

"It takes," he said, "a little more to get me going."

I sat back on my haunches on the bed, hands braced on his hips. He was kneeling in front of me. He kissed me, then asked if I was into fist-fucking. I allowed as how I wasn't exactly, that night.

"Some people find it awfully surgical," he said. His cock was at half-mast now, just from talking about it.

"I'll fuck you," I offered. Some concession.

But my cock didn't seem to be enough.

&

Talking to Joe about the double-consciousness of hot sex—people rapping on the door while I was blowing the guy in the john; that it was a highly erotic situation, but humorous, too; that it was both hot and cool.

"Yeah," Joe says. "I used to think that when we, like, graduated from this I'd want to do hot bookstore sex. Now I don't know. Why make it hard on yourself?"

&

Tonight I jacked off Joe since he was having trouble getting blown, and then, after he'd jacked me off a bit, I picked up my porno and began doing myself. I asked him if he would take my cock in his mouth as I was cumming. I'd had an idea that maybe we could work backward, as we had jerking off, and then gradually work in blowing.

When I was about to cum, I told him, and he took my cum in his mouth.

He swallowed it.

"What's the matter? Don't you like the taste?"
"No. That's not it."
"Did it taste salty? Acrid?"
"No. Just that it's yours."

⚑

I've gone to bed with five different men since Joe and I
started tricking in December. Each time I've ended up
jacking myself off. Joe has been to bed with one, not count-
ing me. He's had the opportunity, God knows. I often
imagine him standing like some facetious Southern belle, in
a Long Island bar, making eyes only at the men who are
obviously unavailable. Not exactly a cocktease, but impervi-
ous to the beaus and potential beaus on either side of him—
out of fear of losing his figurative virginity.
    When *I* do that, I'm very butch.

⚑

Dear ———
Your second letter arrived yesterday, the one from Taos.
The first, from Atlanta, I think we'll have to give up for
dead. Anyway, no one has any idea where you are now
because your Itinerary was obsolete by the time you left
Washington.
    Your letters are so full of what's obviously inspired
invention that I don't know whether to take stories like the
one about the Fundamentalist in Dallas seriously or not.
Do you really go on talk shows and answer questions over
the phone? What is it like being a Famous Author promot-
ing a book? Do you shave for radio?
    We're very depressed by the news that you'll have to
be "on tour" another month. But New York is very gray
anyway. Nothing of note is happening here. You ask for
dish. I don't have any, other than the fact that our femi-
nist friend has taken a house in Rhinebeck, New York, and
is keeping her twenty-three-year-old boy/man up there.

*The house is owned by two old Reds who've gone to Israel
to try out kibbutz life. The dishwasher is kosher and thus
is padlocked, but the house is completely surrounded by
woods and she says she and her boyfriend jog miles every
morning and only eat eggs from chickens who run free
and eat feed without chemicals in it.*

*Our Fire Island friend discarded the High Tech and
took his Biedermeier out of storage.*

*I'm sure you heard all from our dancing friend re:
political friend and demise of their affair. Well, our P.
friend has found a Twinkie. He met him at the baths and
they have had sex twice since then. The Twinkie lives on
East Third Street in a commune with other Twinkies of
assorted sizes, but all, says our friend, essentially indistinguishable from his. I asked him what he saw in the kid,
and he said that when you twist his nipples you get Tokyo
and that's all you have to do.*

*Dancing friend as insouciant as ever. He took me to
Flamingo last night. It wasn't the same, he said, without
you. "Or rather, it is the same. You know? How dreary."*

*I'm sure he wrote you about the riot there two weeks
ago—how they stormed the booth because poor Walter
missed two separate segues between records and how the
staff then locked themselves in the office and how the
rioters forced the lighting man to play the rest of the
evening? Last week, he said, the general atmosphere in
there was like the cease-fire over the Sinai after the Six-
Day War.*

Big Jack (see Honcho *cover for this month) bumped
into me. It was like colliding with a padded cell turned
inside out. I was* very *embarrassed, as Joe would say—he
says "Hi!"—as I fell down. The walls at Fl. were goboed
with big red roses. I saw The Man Who Walks His Dog. He
was wearing* his glasses. *Very courageous.*

*You haven't mentioned word one about sex in either
of your letters. Are you getting any? Do they still do it
West of the Hudson? Or has the fashion caught on Out
There too?*

It was, you see, my impression at Fl. that everyone here would rather not. Maybe it's the winter doldrums. In any case, as I sat there watching the passing parade, I realized that swimming back into what I'd assumed was the mainstream is going to be a chore. You know, I always did feel that my dysfunction was a form of protest, among other things. Against the utter impersonality of the scene (what our dancing friend calls "the Circuit"), the sexual overload in a place like Fl. It was about as sexually stimulating to me as watching new cars roll off an assembly line in Detroit, Michigan. (You'll write that that's *very stimulating to some people.) When I came home and saw myself in the bathroom mirror, I looked like pure Biafra after what I'd been viewing for five hours. (Tell me again, please, that muscles are just a fad.) I don't want to compete. Can't. Give me a salesman from Jersey, in his polyester suit, glimpsed on the street briefly, his shy cruise. . . .*

Is this pure romanticism?

I realize my point of view (P.O.V., as you say in the writing game) is warped by: 1) Living in New York. 2) My disability. But really, I hear no one makes out much anymore. At least not in the old, conventional way.

Please don't advise me as follows: 1) "A body is a precious gift you give to someone you love" — vis-a-vis *muscles. 2) "If you're so infatuated with men in polyester suits from New Jersey, buy one (a suit) and infiltrate." 3) "Take out an ad in the* New York Review of Books.*"*

Love,
Danny

P.S. Our actor friend has just bought an answering machine. It serenades you with three minutes of Brahm's "Fest-und Gedenksprüche" before the beep.

In his therapy group, they were talking about this guy who is having problems with his girlfriend, and Joe, who is usually silent, just started talking about how he had the same problem with a guy he used to see. . . .

Everyone was aghast. Without quite realizing what he was doing, Joe had come out to them. He gleefully described the scene to me.

He is thinking of getting his hair body-waved. He has a hairdresser friend who will do it for him.

⚐

Joe has driven to an unfamiliar town to meet his friend Billy in an unfamiliar bar. It is ten o'clock and the bar is empty but for three or four customers and the bartender. Joe buys a Coke and sits down at a table, out of the way, near the front door.

"Hot place," Billy'd said on the phone.

Billy always has a boyfriend. Joe wonders if he'll show up with the boyfriend tonight. Not like old times, when he and Joe came out—together, with each other. Joe is always jealous of these new boyfriends, even though he's no longer sexually attracted to Billy.

A few more people come in. This is not New York City, and the place fills up early. It's a Wednesday night.

("You're never home nights anymore," his mother has said, her sole comment on the past few months of "practice.")

Billy doesn't come and doesn't come. Joe is getting pissed. It's almost eleven and he's just about decided to leave. A man has been watching him from the bar and he's starting to feel more uncomfortable, sitting there with an empty glass in front of him.

A big, swarthy type, the man comes over to Joe's table. "Mind?" Sits down opposite Joe.

"Billy," he says, extending his hand.

For a moment, Joe thinks this might be some password

or that the man has come here to meet Billy, too, then he dismisses his confusion and shakes the man's—Billy's—hand.

The usual preliminaries, and Joe is in an agony of nerves, looking at the front door and hoping the real Billy will come in after all, trying not to be so friendly to this new Billy as to be encouraging, trying at the same time to look this Billy over.

Billy is very open in his assessment of Joe.

Billy doesn't come here very often himself. He used to go into the City. As a matter of fact, he lived there for a while. But he doesn't go into the City much anymore.

Joe tells Billy what he does for a living, but gives him the name of a different store in a different shopping mall.

Billy is a—gasp—truck driver! (Gulp.) He is thirty-four. To Joe, he looks older than thirty-four.

Billy offers to buy Joe a Coke. He is drinking beer himself.

He returns to the table with Joe's Coke and a fresh beer for himself.

The minutes drag on. Billy is very affable. Billy is, Joe can't help but admit to himself, hot. Billy is also very tenacious.

The place is getting crowded. For someone who doesn't come here very often, Billy certainly knows a lot of people. Billy says hello to an awful lot of people.

"All right," Billy finally says, when it is twelve o'clock. "Here's the deal. I can't take you home with me because I'm living with this chick. But I have this friend who owns a nice hotel and we can go there for free. Wanna?"

Joe crunches down on an ice cube from the third Coke this Billy has bought for him. "I gotta go to the bathroom," Joe says.

"Be my guest," says Billy, making a sweeping gesture with his hand.

Joe goes to the bathroom. He can't decide about Billy. He comes out of the bathroom. He sees that Billy is still at the table. He elbows his way through the crowd in front of the bar, but that doesn't give him enough time to make a decision either. And of course he can't just leave, as Billy is sitting next to the door.

"That shit, that fuckhead," Joe thinks of his old friend, the original Billy.

He sits down opposite the truck driver.

"I want you to sit on my face," says Billy.

"Oh?" (Gulp.)

"I wanna stick my nose up your crack," says Billy.

"Ah." (Gulp.)

Billy sticks out his long, pointed tongue.

"Is this—ah—a really nice hotel?" (Might as well get it over with. . . .) "As nice as you say?"

"Would *I* lie to you?"

"No, I just—"

"I mean, what reason would I have to lie to you?"

Out in the parking lot, Billy says Joe should leave his car there and ride with him. He thinks Joe lives in the town with the other shopping mall and the fictitious job, and he'll "save Joe some time."

"I'll follow you," Joe says very firmly. (Hooray for Joe!)

He follows Billy, in his own car, to a motel.

Billy registers and pays the desk clerk.

Outside the office, Joe says, "Your friend doesn't own this motel at all, does he?"

"Follow me," Billy says.

The room is only a few doors away from the office. There is no time to decide whether to leave or not.

Inside the room, Joe says, "This isn't a nice hotel at all."

"Let me take off your clothes," Billy says. He begins unbuttoning Joe's shirt. Joe feels himself getting hard. "You wouldn't have come here with me if I hadn't lied," Billy says.

"No." (Gulp.)

Billy is very attractive, really. He is a little taller than Joe, but not that much better built, really, and—why does Joe trust him?

Billy sucks Joe's nipple, giving it a loud smack. Then he lets Joe's shirt drop to the floor. His hands slide down Joe's arms and grasp his wrists.

"I'll set the pace," Billy says. "You set the limits."

He places his hand on Joe's chest and gives him a gentle shove. The edge of the mattress hits the backs of Joe's knees. He falls in slow motion onto the bed. Billy unbuckles Joe's belt, unbuttons Joe's jeans, skins the jeans off Joe's hips, rubs his face in Joe's jockey shorts.

"Mmmmm," Billy says from deep in Joe's crotch.

He grabs the elastic waistband and pulls down Joe's shorts. He grabs Joe's balls and twists them. He licks Joe's balls, smooth and hard as they now are, aching, captured in his fist.

"Limit," Joe whispers.

Billy straightens up and smiles. "You really afraid, or just pretending?"

"I'm really afraid," Joe admits.

"Oh, I'm sorry," Billy says, evidently sincere, contrite. "You've never done the leather scene, have you?"

(Gulp.)

"No," Joe whispers.

"What?"

Joe clears his throat. "No, I haven't."

"Turn over, baby."

Billy buries his face, as promised, in Joe's ass.

"Turn out the light, baby."

"Can we leave it on?"

"Let's turn it off."

Joe reaches up and turns out the bedside lamp.

Billy stands next to the bed and slowly takes off his clothes, down to his boxer shorts.

"I wanna fuck you, okay?"

Joe can see how magnificent Billy's chest is, in the light from the parking lot.

"You don't really live with a chick, do you?"

"Sure. She's Italian. Just like you."

"Oh."

"But I like a man, too."

Billy takes off his boxer shorts. His cock is limp.

Billy sticks his tongue up Joe's ass, farther, farther, beyond the point where Joe thought anyone's tongue could ever go. Billy licks and sucks. His hand goes between Joe's legs and under him, to Joe's cock.

"Oh, baby," Billy moans.

"Oh," Joe moans. Nevertheless, when *two* of Billy's fingers work into his asshole, Joe bolts at the intrusion. Just think dildo, Joe counsels himself. But Billy's *three* fingers are neither the shape nor size of Joe's trusty dildo.

Billy turns Joe over, lies full length on top of him, tongues Joe's mouth. Joe is very hard. He has been very hard since Billy let loose of his balls, near the beginning.

Billy is hard now, too.

Billy sits up between Joe's legs, spits in his hand and smooths it over his cock, puts his arms under Joe's legs, lifts the legs up in the crooks of his arms, lifts Joe's ass off the bed, hunkers down between Joe's thighs, reaches under to grasp his own cock, brings it to the rim of Joe's asshole, presses, pushes, enters slowly, spits on Joe's cock, rubs it with the other hand, shoves in farther. . . .

"Do yourself," he says to Joe, holding Joe's asscheeks in his big hands.

"Oh." Joe rubs his cock, then wraps his hand around it, begins to jack himself.

Billy bends down and kisses Joe on the mouth. It is a big, romantic kiss.

"Never been fucked like a woman, have you?" Billy gasps.

"I'm not a woman." (Hooray for Joe!)

"Baby, that's just dirty talk."

In, out, in, out, like a seesaw.

Joe jacks and jacks and jacks. Billy's pelvis slaps against his upturned ass. Joe jacks and jacks and jacks. When he cums (Hooray for Joe!), he cums with his eyes closed, concentrating on the cock inside him, thinking how he's going to call his friend Billy tomorrow and tell him what a fuckhead he is for not showing up at the bar. . . .

When Joe cums, Billy groans, "Oh, that hurts. That pinches." Joe's sphincter is nipping Billy's cock. "Don't bite if off, man."

"Would *I* do that?" Joe pants.

A

Tonight I brought up my theory about jacking and blowing to Virgil—that maybe we can sneak blowing in, as it isn't working when Joe tries to blow me. Virgil said it might be a good idea.

But instead of feeling optimistic about it as I had, I felt depressed. I knew it wouldn't work but I didn't want to say so.

Virgil asked me what was wrong.

"I don't know," I said. "It's just that—well, Joe doesn't really like to blow me. I know he doesn't. Whether it's me or blowing, I don't know."

"Is that true?" Virgil asked Joe.

Joe pressed his lips together and frowned. "No," he half whispered finally.

"It's not true."

"No. I don't like blowing him."

Joe looked as if he might cry. He said it was his fault I wasn't cumming.

"That's not true," I said. "I don't even know if I like being blown. You don't even know if you'd like blowing someone else. You've gotten very good at it, you know."

But he still looked as if he might cry.

Virgil asked if he was doing a guilt trip on himself.

"What will we do now?" Joe asked. "If we don't blow?"

"Maybe blowing isn't Danny's thing," Virgil said. He turned to me and suggested that I might see Sammy again. That brightened me up considerably. It was a way to practice blowing without all of the other pressures of tricking. And I knew it was *definitely* Sammy's thing, among scores of others.

"Perhaps, then," Virgil said, more tentative than usual, "we should think about terminating. . . . You're still doing a guilt trip on yourself. Aren't you?" he said to Joe.

I think it was the word "terminating" more than our mechanical problem that had Joe upset. Later on, we talked about it, and he was calmer. He felt, when Virgil said that, as if the rug had been pulled out from under his feet.

"I won't know what to do without our practicing," he said. "I don't have anything to take its place."

And he doesn't. But surely he knew that I was still going to be with him until he felt ready to end it?

"I didn't know that," he said. "How do *you* feel about it?" he asked rather abruptly.

I had to admit that I was happy.

"The only thing," he said, "is that I hoped that we would get blowing down until I could cum easy with you blowing me, without your hand."

"We've done that."

"Not really."

"Why is it so important?" I asked.

"It's silly, I know. But I felt that if you could blow me and I could cum, then with the next guy, he could blow me and use his hand at the same time and I would cum that way."

I laughed and asked him how he was going to fit everything that happened in bed with someone else into that kind of program. He laughed too, but I know—just as I know that he's obsessed with the orderly completion of his three-point therapy strategy—that he won't rest easy until his hidden agenda is fulfilled.

I blew him and he came easily. Without my hand.

◬

Dear ———

Your letter from San Francisco was hair-raising. I passed it around. That night, our political friend and I were out on the streets, too. We went down to Sheridan Square. There must have been about five hundred faggots there— and TV, the whole bit. There were some speeches, all very sober and tearful. Of course the most craven among the politicos seemed to feel they'd at last found a martyr in Harvey Milk. I suppose they have. But as you said, we have plenty of martyrs already, we just don't know most of their names. . . .

Your new boyfriend came over for tea last Sunday and we both praised you to the skies for hours. Really. We talked only about you, as a substitute, I think for your company.

I got my hair cut. Very short. It's a big hit. Someone told me I look like someone who might tie up a person but would also quote Whitman to him.

Joe is in good spirits. He got fucked by a truck driver. We are going to "terminate" (Virgil's term) and it's lifted a burden. I was happy at first, but it makes me unaccountably sad, too. I think we had the idea that we would be sexual gymnasts by the end of this, but we had only a brief flirtation with fucking—I'll tell all when you come home.

This is a terrible letter. Life's stopped short. Maybe it was the assassination. Remember when we went down and gave blood after the Everard fire? And you said you felt as if your blood was literally flowing into the veins of the victims upstairs in the hospital? That there must be such a thing as gay blood?

Remember how we all danced at the Firehouse?

You're dead right about Flamingo, of course—that it's a shrine to impersonality and what's wrong with that? I am always looking under rocks for something to slither out, so naturally I find it. I'll do as you say the next time I go, and "try to be nothing but a hot number." There's virtue in that, too.

Our political friend says that all is merely a holding action, and that if we don't learn to relate gently and in a non-sexist manner to each other now, no one will ever learn how to.

I've tricked a bit and I'm certainly not the only one. The other night I went to bed with a twenty-year-old. Just the kind of proposition that would have been so risky in the past. He was as passive and unsure as I was. He didn't really know how to kiss. I pretended I didn't know how to do anything, *this after I touched his butt and he flinched, so I knew he was most terrified of that. We had, then, prep-school sex. He very sweetly put his tongue in my ear and, while I jacked myself off, I suddenly saw us as what we were (in my mind's eye): a fearful child and an older man whose primary gift was patience and understanding. He is a student at Columbia. He wouldn't give me his phone number, which was all right.*

I'm enclosing a dirty book which I bought for you at the dirty bookstore. (I didn't, as you suggested, go into the back for a quickie in the stalls.) I hope Manhandler assuages your loneliness somewhat. In which city do you think you picked up the clap? Dallas? I'm sure that in San Francisco you can get an injection anywhere. Even while standing on line to pay the light bill. They're so community-minded out there, God bless them.

Love,
Danny

＾

Long session with Sammy. I learned a lot—especially when I kept my eyes open and watched what he was doing. But when I was doing that, there was no chance I would cum. And when I wasn't watching and could forget it was Sammy doing those things to me, cumming seemed close yet far.

At one point, he came up for air and stretched out beside me. He asked me how I felt.

"I don't know," I lied, ashamed to admit that I wasn't feeling anything—and if you can't with Sammy, then with whom?

"Frustrating. Isn't it?" he said.

"Yeah."

"You could have, I *think*, cum three or four times there, but I didn't make you."

My eyes popped open. "Why?"

"Well, I wasn't sure. But you wouldn't tell me you wanted to. You wouldn't say, 'Keep that up' or 'Don't stop that.' You were like a bump on a log."

A

"What more can I do for you?" Virgil asked me.

I told him I wasn't sure I liked being blown that much. (I hadn't cum that way with Sammy.) But that I'd find out with other people. I felt it now, more than I was ever able to before. That it was enjoyable.

"What can I do for you in terms of sex therapy?"

I was taken aback by the question. FINIS was written in the air before my eyes.

"I don't know," I fumbled. "I'm thinking of—larger issues. Relationships. Being in love. Letting someone in." I was conscious that I was smirking. "Be here," I said, in answer to his question, "when they come up. When I meet someone. I *would* like to know that I can cum without having to jack myself off. I suppose I will, in time."

He smiled. I couldn't read the expression in his eyes; the light was reflecting in a glare off his glasses. But I felt a sinking feeling and knew I'd just been gently nudged out of the nest and was falling. . . .

A

Dream of Max: Christmas Eve. The Christmas we spent together, I sense. We are in a fancy restaurant having dinner. We can find nothing to say. Max's acute embarrassment over this makes it more painful. I am ready to cry. I excuse myself and go to the john. In the john I ponder whether I should just leave Max there. "He has the money." Just walk out.

Max comes into the john. There are dividers, plate glass, between the basins. I am washing my hands. Max leans over the basin and takes out a jackknife. He begins hacking at his wrists. I yell at him, search for a way around the glass divider, but it runs wall to wall, floor to ceiling. There is a phone, like the phones that divide prisoners from their visitors. I pick up the phone. Max keeps hacking. Blood is oozing into the basin under his wrists. He is concentrating on hacking away at his wrists with the same complete concentration he had when working.

I jiggle the receiver, pound on the plate glass, yell and scream for him to forgive me, but he doesn't look up. It is a long and difficult job as the blood will not flow freely.

The dream ends.

A

Virgil says Joe doesn't have a sexual problem—"All the equipment is working"—but a social problem. Assertiveness. "For that, I can't help you," he says. "It's not my thing, really." He suggests that Joe take some kind of assertiveness training.

"Every faggot in the world needs that," I told Joe later, conveniently forgetting the famous faggots who I know live to play football and, like Lord Kitchener, wage wars.

"Cruising school?" Joe speculated.

A

As Virgil took us to the door the other night, he said, "And when you get out there and start to trick again, you'll find there are so many dysfunctional guys. . . ." Like an exterminator who has to go out and face all the roaches in the city, whose work is never done.

⚠

Virgil says one thing made us successful, and that was
that we were open enough at the first to take a chance on
each other, were not chained to rigid likes and dislikes about
partners. He says it's hard for him to "match" people who
only like men with mustaches and big tits and big cocks, or
whatever. That their preferences are really often part of the
problem.

⚠

Dream of Max: Sitting out on a long pier, Province-
town-like setting, him on my lap. In love with him as I was at
first. He was wearing a red tank suit. Ran my fingers down
his arm and he shivered. Butt squirmed against my hardon.
All the time conversing with women of our acquaintance.
Tall, cool drinks in our hands.

(That was it. Of course, my wet dreams are never "wet"
—only once, when I was twelve or so. But this was very close
to one. I remember how I used to hold my cock when I was
cumming, when a teenager at home, so I wouldn't foul the
sheets. Joe says this is why I squirt. Wonder if it's why I don't
have wet dreams.)

⚠

I remember being in love with Max. I remember walking down Fifth Avenue one noon hour, in front of the
Public Library, with the heat rising up off the sidewalk
around me and people streaming past me, office workers
coming and going with shopping bags and parcels and
balloons and ice cream cones, tourists taking pictures of
each other in front of the stone lions, venders hawking
plastic belts and jewelry, boys on the corners snapping
massage-parlor fliers and rapping "Check it out," a saxophone player riffing "Satin Doll" at the foot of the steps,
and behind him tiers upon tiers of sweating, gesticulating,

laughing, cracked, sunstroked people. And all I could think of was Max, and that Max was somewhere uptown, and Max was the Max I loved.

⚑

  After I broke up with Max I lost a lot of weight, my mustache went gray, I looked old. One night, walking down the street, my political friend touched my arm. We stopped and he said to me, "One of these days, Danny, you're going to be able to see yourself as—well, as a person who got shit on but survived. That day will come. I promise."

⚑

Dear ———

I've copied out and pasted up on my bathroom mirror your quotation:

> *The aim of therapy is to convert neurotic suffering into ordinary human misery.*

  Friday night as I write this. Hoots and howls outside my window. We've hit a warm spell and the tourists are out in full force. The park is Bongo City. I have no desire to go out tonight. I watched TV a little, read, listened to music.
  I picked up a lawyer *at the Cockring last weekend. He insisted on fucking me and when I said no (didn't at all like the insistence), he said, "Well, what will we do, then?" We finally said, Oh, forget it, and he left.*
  My mother called the next day and said my father is very ill again and had to have an operation the day before—very complicated, getting out the news—and that they'd had to castrate him. She was holding up well, as usual. We talked a long time, then I hung up and sort of

caved in for a while. She didn't want me to come, which is just as well, I think. He is home now, though bedridden, of course. She says at his age and after his hormone treatments he doesn't seem to care that much. But I wondered.

You'll ask me how it feels, to have my father lose his balls. It's supposed to be such an Oedipal dream, isn't it? Well, I'm not sure. But I'm beyond all those mixed feelings now, I think. Just frustrated not to see him, not to be of any earthly help.

On to cheerier things. Joe has registered for asser-tiveness training *(Virgil recommended it) at the local junior college. The fact that he didn't say one word in the first class might indicate to you that he has a problem. He's going in order to learn how to cruise, but the only exercise in the curriculum that seems to apply to his particular situation at all is asking a stranger for the time of day. . . .*

Our Fire Island friend is in danger of losing his house this year. The owner says he's going to renovate it, and we're sure he'll turn it into Love American Style *with a whole other floor and a warren of little rooms.*

Our dancing friend has restricted his pastime to the Cockring on Thursday nights. He says the music every-where else is for shit. For the first time since we've known him, he looks well and rested. He must be telling the truth and not sneaking uptown to that Spanish place as I sus-pected.

No, I didn't find it "impossible to keep my hands off of" your boyfriend. He is not my type and he seems determined to be utterly faithful to you. What's your secret? Cucumber cream?

Our actor friend introduced me to a new buddy of his the other night. They're appearing together Off-Off-Broadway in a revival of The Corn Is Green *("All of us call it just plain* Corn*"). His new buddy is very attrac-tive, just moved down to the Village last year, has a big, very attractive, very black lover—and a dog. Give up?*

He didn't recognize me as I was wearing my new contact lenses.

Our political friend and his neighbors are organizing to build a windmill on his tenement roof.

Time to turn in. We are chaste, aren't we? Me with my Wyndham Lewis and you with your social disease. (I told you to get an injection in S.F.—and now you have all Chicago at your feet, and nothing.) Has anyone in Chicago burned a cross in front of your hotel door yet? Lock it and put a chair under the knob. We want you home intact. A "Commie" is the last thing I'd call you. What are those talk-show callers thinking of?

Love,
Danny

P.S.: Our actor friend's answering machine now plays a brief excerpt from "Granados y Camiña's Goyescas," rendered by Alicia de Larrocha. Then his lover's voice comes on and identifies the selection as "Arroya con Pollo" by Alice Roach. The beep is gone altogether.

A

Dream of Max (Came down with such finality, I woke with a start at the end): We are in our apartment with a view of apartment house spires and the park to the south. It is twilight. I am in the front bedroom and walk to the door, look down the long hall. Max is passing back and forth across the hall from one room to another (rooms that never existed in such abundance in our real apartment), and I watch him tiptoeing across the hall.

I walk back into the little bedroom. It is bare and dark, only the light from the airshaft. In that bare gray room I shout, "Max!" Once. A command.

I imagine him, arrested in the center of the hall, weight poised on one foot, frightened, indecisive. But he must come to me.

He enters the room slowly, tentatively. I turn to face him to. . . .

("Kill him, of course," says my Fire Island friend.)

Friends," said dear Thoreau. "They are like air bubbles on water, hastening to flow together. . . ."

⚚

"Darling, it's just too wonderful to be back. Manhattan couldn't be more beautiful. Driving back into midtown over the bridge last night, in fact, it was a gross parody of itself. Like your beloved Gershwin's "Rhapsody in Blue" sung by the Mormon Tabernacle Choir. But I *will* miss America. The trip was *so* broadening. Everyone out there is really *so* nice. They tell you *everything* about themselves on the basis of a mere handshake or a seat shared on the bus. Not like *us* at all, with our appointment books and our mania for privacy, our vulgar late-night confessions. . . .

"But when can we see each other? Let me get my little book. Are you free Mondays now? Is the therapy over? Oh, too bad. I was hoping that you would be graduated by now. Darling, it's just like psychoanalysis or something. Or *dialysis*. Oh, you know I have tickets to the ballet for next Wednesday. Baryshnikov. Want to go? Wonderful. . . .

"Shall we meet for drinks before? But where? Oh, I seem to have a date for drinks. Well, we'll meet at O'Neal's across the street. I'll just stay put. Oh, no, can't. I'll *have* to be downtown. Perhaps we should just meet on the plaza, but if the weather's foul we can meet at the main entrance. No, that's no good, I always miss you there. We *could* meet at our seats. That's it. But I can't—find the tickets. Oh, darling, I haven't the tickets. I should be able to get your ticket *to* you. Let's see, I could drop it off Sunday. No, that's out. I'm going to Brookville—or is that *next* weekend? Well, you'll just have to come by for tea tomorrow after work, pick up your ticket and. . . .

"Splendid. Oh, darling, you're just a wizard at these things, aren't you? Okay. Tomorrow, shall we say around five-thirty? Or will that give you enough time? Oh, dear, *I'll* be *midtown*, I see, at five. We could meet *midtown*, for a drink. . . ."

A

"God, I'm sorry, Danny. I completely forgot about it. Can you find someone else to go with you? We're having a meeting here about the windmill and since I'm. . . .

"What? I can't hear you. Everyone's talking. . . .

"But how many times does *The Gang's All Here* come around?. . . .

"Well, okay. Did you know that if you generate too much electricity with one of these things you have to give it to Con Ed? This is impossible, Danny. Can't hear a thing. I'll call you tomorrow. Promise. And, sorry. . . ."

A

"Oh, I'm sorry, babe, I can't. Marcella's coming over to coach me for 'The $20,000 Pyramid.' I'm going on this Monday! I'm supposed to be a bank clerk, which of course I've *been* and probably will be again, but the show is just riddled with actors, they say. The auditions were grueling.

We've already spent the money, of course. Europe. Wanna come to Europe with us? And cable TV. I'm going to buy a big color TV set and a new suit and we're going to repaint the kitchen. . . .

"After the taping. Super. I'll tell you *everything*. And keep your fingers crossed. Pray to Goodson and Todman. And throw in one to Procter and Gamble while you're at it. . . ."

A

"Danny, I know you're just going to hate us for this, but the pump just conked out and we can't make it. The basement is hip-high in water and the furnace went off and it's freezing up here. We're wearing every stitch of clothing we have and we can't get the repairman and it's started snowing. Is it snowing in the City? Randy's crawling around down there with a flashlight and I know he's going to electrocute himself or something. He won't listen to *me*, of course. Oh, God! Oh, Danny, he fell in! Have to get off. Call me. Or I'll. . . . Oh, my God! Men! . . ."

A

"Hi, I'm not in right now. I'm out assembling my costume for the Tropicana party. At the sound of the beep, you may leave a message and any fashion tips you might have. Keep in mind that poison green clashes with my eyes. . . ."

A

"Hey, Danny," said my Fire Island friend.
"You sound awful. What's wrong?"
"Flu."
"How awful. When'd *that* happen?"
"Somewhere between the Glory Hole and the Catacombs last night."
"Do you need anything?"

"No, I'm lying on the couch, listening to Scriabin, and I just put a chicken on to boil."

"Sure?"

"Yeah, honey. Thanks. Oh, I got my house back."

"For the whole summer?"

"Yeah, he just called today. He's putting off the renovations."

"That's great!"

"Yeah." He hacked into the receiver. "It's this fucking weather," he said.

"Yeah," I said.

"What are you up to?" he asked.

"At loose ends. I think I'll stay home tonight and clean the bathroom."

"You're always cleaning the bathroom."

"I have the cleanest bathroom in New York."

"You're terrific husband material," he said.

"I know," I said. "I'll call you tomorrow. Not too early."

"I had to break a terrific fuck date," he said.

"You *must* be sick."

ᐃ

"What *are* you doing, Danny?"

"What do you mean, what am I doing? I'm cleaning the bathroom. What are *you* doing here?"

My political friend and my actor friend exchange exasperated looks, push past me into the apartment.

"Well, there's no time for a shower," says my actor friend, taking my coat off the hook.

"No, he'll just have to go the way he is," says my political friend. He looks down at my feet. "*Please*, Danny. Put your shoes on. We don't have any time. We're late already!"

My actor friend helps me into my coat.

"For what?" I ask, attempting to get into the spirit of the thing.

"Do put down that sponge, Danny," says my actor friend.

"Where are we going? Can't I at least put in my contacts?"

"No time," says my political friend, shoe poised under my foot.

"Where's your script?" asks my actor friend.

"Script?"

"Lift," says my political friend.

He ties my shoelaces.

"Well, I don't suppose it matters at this point," says my actor friend, bustling about, turning off the lights. "You *do* know your lines, don't you?"

"Lines?"

"Button up," says my political friend.

"His hair's a mess," observes my actor friend.

"What lines?" What script? What kind of practical joke is this?

They hustle me downstairs. It is lightly raining outside. A taxi is waiting at the curb. They bundle me into the taxi. We speed off down the street.

"Maybe you could tell me what this is all about," I venture when we've turned onto Sixth Avenue and are on our way uptown.

"Stage fright," my actor friend says, leaning across me, to my political friend.

"Fear of flying," agrees my political friend. He pats my hand. "You'll be fine, Danny. Just relax."

The tires slap against the wet pavement. The windshield wipers swish, clunk. Neon wiggles across the windows.

"But really," I say.

The taxi is shaken by a series of potholes.

"Ouch," I complain. "I bit my tongue."

"Any excuse," says my political friend to my actor friend.

"Any," agrees my actor friend.

"But weawly," I say.

"Left! Left!" cries my actor friend, as we almost overshoot an intersection. The taxi careens down a side street, splattering passersby.

We come to a shattering halt in front of the theater.

"I'll pay," says my political friend, pushing me across the seat. My actor friend seizes my hand and yanks me onto the sidewalk. He pulls me into a side door marked only RICO 198 and CASTRATE RAPISTS. He pushes me down a black corridor. We emerge into a greenroom.

"Not that way," he says to me, taking my arm. He takes me down another hallway and drags me into a dressing room.

"What *is* this all—"

"Sit down, sit down. We have *ten* minutes. Here, take off your coat. Oh, your hair!"

My Fire Island friend sticks his head in the door.

"At last! Jesus, Danny, where have you *been?*"

"I was cleaning the—"

But my actor friend is smearing cold cream over my face.

"The lighting's completely fucked up," says my Fire Island friend.

"Not my department," says my actor friend, wiping off the cold cream with tissues.

"Hey, you're getting it all over my—"

"Close your mouth, Danny."

"These queens don't know what the fuck they're doing," groans my Fire Island friend, disappearing down the hallway.

An argument from the next room:

"So? What? I don't know how to use an iron?"

"It's just that no one wears jeans *pressed.*" It's my feminist friend.

"So we can't just iron out the crease?" says Molly Goldberg. "We can't just give them a little sprinkle?"

"No one listens to *me*," says Lillian Gish, sweet but a tad petulant.

"Why don't we—" begins my feminist friend.

"Darling," says Molly. "Go back to your amplifiers and microphones. *That* you know about."

My actor friend is wetting down my hair with a spritz bottle.

"I would really like to know—"

"Who has the blow dryer!" he shrieks, rummaging through the makeup and tissues on the table. "Blot," he says to me, throwing a towel over my head. "Blot."

"I really—"

"Where's Richie!" screams my dancing friend from the hall. "Where's Richie!" It echoes down the corridor.

"Darling. . . ." It's my novelist friend, at my ear.

"What *is* this—"

"Darling, I've put in some additional material. Don't panic. I've written it out on little three-by-five cards. Just try to do the lines with—oh, I'd say a kind of saucy insouciance. Think Ann-Margret."

"Do you mind?" says my actor friend, snatching the towel off my head. He is armed with makeup sticks.

"And I've been thinking about that little speech at the end of the first act," says my novelist friend.

My actor friend lays down a greasepaint base.

"I think just a *teensy* bit more butch. You know." My novelist friend makes a delicate gesture in the mirror. "Not Clint Eastwood. More like Burt Reynolds. With the slightest undercurrent of irony. Just a touch of humor before the really wrenching passage. . . ."

"Please, Danny. Hold still."

"But I don't even—"

"I think that's about it," says my novelist friend, consulting a clipboard. "I'm sure you'll be *wonderful*. And remember. The word is 'facade,' but without the cedilla. I know you'll think it's affected but—"

"Close your eyes, Danny."

"Where *is* Richie!"

"Demonstrators!" I can hear my political friend scream. "Demonstrators?"

"Isn't that a bit dark?" says my novelist friend. "This isn't a silent film, you know."

"Go away, go away," says my actor friend, daubing at my eyelids.

"Break a leg, Danny."

"He'll be fine. It's just the jitters."

"And that speech in the—"

"*Please*," begs my actor friend.

He works in silence for a while. The Righteous Brothers' "You've Lost That Lovin' Feeling" booms from the offstage speakers.

"No no no!" screams my dancing friend, far away. "We decided on 'I Will Survive'!"

My actor friend assaults my face with a powder puff. I gasp and cough. "Close your mouth," he says.

"Five minutes," says my Fire Island friend from the doorway.

"Jesus, Mary, and Joseph," moans my actor friend.

"Danny, just one thing," says my Fire Island friend, squatting beside me. "Don't try to pick up the bottle. The bottle's glued down. It's a quick scene change and we had to glue it down."

"He knows."

What bottle?

"What are you doing to his lips?"

"Look, you stick to your—"

"You're giving him bee-stung lips."

"This is THE THEATRE. I should know lips," my actor friend snaps.

"Uh, excuse me," says a deep bass voice from the door. We all look in the mirror. It is Captain O'Malley. He is dressed in a white shirt, open at the collar, and a blue business suit. He holds a little bouquet of daisies in his hand.

"I wanted to wish you luck," he says shyly, casting his eyes to the floor.

"Why, thank you," I say, dumfounded. "But *I* really don't—"

"I'm sure you'll be just great," he says, handing the flowers to my Fire Island friend and disappearing.

"Who was *that*?" breathes my actor friend.

"The Gay Activists Alliance is demonstrating in front of the theater!" screams my political friend from somewhere.

"Here we are," chimes Molly Goldberg, sweeping into the room with a pair of jeans over her arm. "Nice and clean, freshly pressed."

There is a distant crash. My Fire Island friend gasps and exits.

My actor friend is running liner under my eyes.

Molly picks up a comb and does my hair.

"No part," instructs my actor friend.

"No part?"

"God, no. *No one* wears a part anymore. Fluff it up."

"Such pretty hair." She leans close. "You'll be fine, *bubalah*. Just remember who you are." She gives my cheek a pat and goes out.

My actor friend works frantically on my hair for a few moments. Then he stands behind me with my head in his hands and turns my face from side to side, examining his work in the mirror.

"This is a dream," I say to him through bee-stung lips. "Isn't it?"

"It'll just have to do."

"Three minutes," calls my Fire Island friend.

I pull on the jeans, which are a size too small. I am buttoning up the flannel shirt when my dancing friend sticks his head in the door.

"You're not putting *that* on him, are you?"

"Not my department," says my actor friend, washing his hands at the little sink.

"Not *flannel*!"

"What's wrong with it?" asks my Fire Island friend, behind him.

"I *specified* flannel. In the script," says my novelist friend, rushing in with a sheet of paper on which the ink is still wet. "Danny, I've just rewritten—"

"Flannel! That's *so* tired. He'll look like a clone!"

"I've just rewritten—"

"You have makeup on your collar."

"Two minutes," says my Fire Island friend. "Where *is* that lighting queen?" he says, running off.

"Just a little T-shirt. You can't possibly *dance* in flannel."

"I wanted an ordinary guy. I want him to look like just a plain—"

"Look out for your eyes! You're going to smudge them!"

"A guinea T."

"Too ethnic."

"Has anyone seen my duckbilled pliers?" yells my feminist friend.

From the speakers come the opening bars of Streisand's "La Vie En Rose."

"Not that!" shrieks my dancing friend, leaping out of the room.

"You look fine," my actor friend reassures me.

"Just remember your objectives," says my novelist friend. "Let's just run over your objectives, real quick—"

"One minute!"

My actor friend takes me by the shoulders and steers me into the hall.

"Saucy insouciance!" my novelist friend calls after us.

The hallway is dark, lighted by the usual twenty-five-watt bulbs. He takes me up a flight of metal stairs and out into the wings. He plants me offstage, next to a torture rack constructed out of papier-mâché. . . .

"Hi," someone says to me, shaking my hand. A short, bearded guy in a gray corduroy suit. "We've never met, have we? At least not officially. Hank." He pumps my hand. "Very exciting, isn't it?" he says, looking out onto the stage with bright eyes. My Fire Island friend is directing a swarm of stagehands.

"I really don't know what I'm—" I begin.

"Oh, you'll be fine, really. Bill couldn't make it, by the way, but he'll be at the party after. Sends his regrets."

"You're. . . ."

"Yes?"

"You're . . . oh, this is *such* an honor," I stammer.

"Listen. I'm glad you pulled yourself out of that awful funk," Thoreau says. "Won't do at all. Take it from me. I've been there," he says, bouncing on the balls of his feet.

A live orchestra is tuning up in the pit. I can make out snatches of "Cry Me a River."

"But you," I say. "You were a *loner.*"

"Oh, I know," he says, biting his lower lip and smiling ruefully. "I wrote, 'In your higher moods what man is there to meet? You are of necessity isolated.' Bullshit. All of it. I was just as lonely as the next guy."

My Fire Island friend is clearing the stage. My feminist friend is crawling along the curtain line, checking out microphone cords. My novelist friend is fidgeting in the wings, making signs at me across the vast space that separates us. I turn to Hank, to say something, but he's gone.

"But where's Joe?" I ask.

The orchestra strikes up "Another Opening, Another Show"—to a disco beat.

"But where's Joe?"

My voice is tiny in the yawning expanse. The stage is cleared now. The orchestra swings into a flamenco version of "Strangers in the Night," augmented by a taped *salsa* rhythm section.

"Where's Joe?"

My cry is a child's cry, plaintive.

The orchestra reaches a crescendo on the last notes of "I Cover the Waterfront." My knees are knocking together. A rivulet of sweat is running down my spine, into the crack of my butt.

My contact lenses! How will I see the audience? What lines? What three-by-five cards? What bottle? Saucy insouciance? I check my fly.

The curtain is rising noiselessly. The footlights are dimming to blackout. A single spot hits the center of the stage. I turn and look about me. The wings are empty. I look across the stage, where the white fall of the spotlight burns on the boards. The tiny red lights on the amps and over the stage-manager's booth wink at me like ship lights far out at sea. There is not a murmur, not a stir from beyond the apron. All is inky blackness out there.

"But where's Joe?" I whisper.

⚑

Once, about a year ago, when he got tired of hearing me talk and talk and talk, I guess, Virgil suggested we have a "nonverbal" session. The next time I came in, a variety of objects was set out on the floor; Virgil told me to sit there and play with them, "relate to them."

I sat down, feeling thoroughly silly, and began to sort them out in my methodical fashion: a typewriter ribbon; several notepads; pencils; paper clips; a piece of two-by-four; a buffer, the kind you attach to a drill; a rubber glove of the black, plumbers' variety; a hammer; a small Tensor lamp; a length of lamp cord; a watch; Virgil's passport, which I read with impertinent interest; a letter from Virgil's publisher; various other things. By the time I got done sorting, I had completely compartmentalized my life according to job, etc.—as I'd attached private meanings to each object there.

I began to assemble a figure out of the cord and wire and so forth. I was very conscious of being allowed to play like this under the indulgent eye of an indulgent papa, a papa who would allow me to read his passport and private correspondence. (My own father was symbolically tucked away in a cardboard box and set aside—I'd put the tools and glove into it.)

"All right," Virgil said when I'd finished the figure.

"Is that all?" I looked up at him from the floor.

"No. Have a seat. What have you made?"

"Warmed-over Picasso," I said, shrugging and looking at the little two-dimensional man on the floor.

"Describe him for me."

"He's . . . dressing for something," I said. "The buffer is like . . . he's making up. To go onstage. The buffer is like a powder puff. And that spool is a mirror. And that lamp, in his third hand"—I shrugged again and smiled—"is like a spotlight. I just thought of something."

"What?" he asked, when I went no further.

I was aware of the blood rising up the back of my neck to my face, that my hands were tingling.

"When I was little, I used to perform for my parents. I used to push the furniture around and dress up in a grass skirt and sing "Little Grass Shack" for them and their friends, in the living room. I was a showoff. Once. I would put on shows. And sing."

"Like him?" Virgil indicated the figure.

I looked down at it. "Yes," I said. A great sadness came over me.

"What are you feeling?"

Standard question. But I didn't know. "Sadness?"

"At what?"

My eyes were riveted on the little figure. It seemed to take on body, a personality greater than its absurd parts.

"I feel sorry for him."

"Why?"

"I don't know."

"Why don't you talk to him?"

I began to. At first I felt absurd, but then I remembered papa would allow me this indulgence. And I knew the little man was me. But I talked to him and told him I was sorry for him. And afraid.

"Tell him why you're afraid for him," Virgil said.

"I'm afraid for you," I began, then tears brimmed in my eyes. "I'm afraid for you because you have to go out there and sing and dance for them. Perform. And you're such a frail, little thing. And the world is . . . cruel." I shot a look up at Virgil. Something was exploding at the back of my head.

"You know," I said, more like myself again, "I can imagine them all sitting there, in those overstuffed chairs, all of them. And their faces are . . .rapacious . . .as they're waiting, and they have long teeth. They won't be easy to please."

⚠

Of course I don't need Virgil to father me anymore. We're past that particular point in therapy. I realized when I could feel sorry for my thirteen-year-old self, with the hypnotist, that I could father myself, in a quite classic and clichéd way. And, of course, that my own father did the best he could, just as I will with him, as much as he'll let me—as much as I had let him.

I'm on the brink now, in the wings. One step and I'll be out on the stage, once again. Is it the old stage fright? This trembling inside? They call it performance anxiety. Stage fright, fear of flying, performance anxiety—it doesn't matter. That first step is the worst.

⚠

Tonight Joe and I sit in Julius, in the back, having a beer and talking. Joe's towels are in my closet at home. His shampoo is sitting on the edge of the tub in the bathroom. His *Man's Image Calendar* is in the bottom drawer of my bureau. I can imagine the awkward ceremony that will accompany my handing them back to him. I don't know when that will be.

Appropriately enough, we're back here, where it seems only lovers and buddies with no need or thought of cruising sit, in this dark back room with its autographed walls and ceilings—what generations of men?—oilcloth on the table tops, quiet conversations between lovers and buddies. When we came through the bar in front, I recognized three men I've slept with, once each, in the past.

Every time I look at Joe, I get a little shock. He had his hair curled, sort of an Italian afro.

Next week he's getting his nose fixed.

Last weekend he drove in with some friends and went to Tea Dance at the Ice Palace. I'm trying to turn him on to a new bar called Hell. I know he'd really shine there. "We can go to Hell," I quip.

He still hasn't gotten laid, and neither have I for quite a while. (Those larger issues I alluded to with Virgil.) I think I'll quit my group therapy soon. My Fire Island friend had me throw the *I Ching* last week and, since it told me essentially what I wanted to hear, I was happy with the results: I am moving out of Stagnation into Passive Change. "You will need the help of friends and associates. Don't force anything. Let change take you where it will."

There was no question of "practice" tonight. As soon as we left Virgil's, Joe said, "Where ya wanna go?" So we came here.

It is over. We both know it.

New York City
July 1978—March 1979

AUTHOR'S AFTERWORD

The Confessions of Danny Slocum began its life in 1979 as an article for *Christopher Street* magazine, intended to be a relatively straightforward (but pseudonymous) account of my own course of sex therapy. When the article was in galleys, Michael Denneny at St. Martin's Press suggested that I expand it into a book and I readily agreed. Although from the first I'd used fictional techniques to tell Danny's story— mainly in order to protect my partner's privacy as well as mine— it took me a while to realize that what was evolving out of the original material was not so much a piece of autobiographical journalism as it was a full-blown novel. So what you have in your hands is one of those literary hybrids, not quite the-whole-truth-and-nothing-but-the-truth in the standard tradition of confessional literature but, I hope, an honest attempt to portray a slice of life at a particular time and in a particular place, however fictionalized the characters or highly-colored the locales might be.

By the time the novel was published with my own name on the cover, I had successfully finished sex therapy and Danny himself had not only ceased to be my alter ego, I had begun to regard him rather as a younger brother, one I wanted to help along in the world but who ultimately would have to stand on his own two feet. These fine distinctions, of course, weren't always appreciated by the people who had read my book and were meeting me for the first time . . .

The book received some good reviews, had a decent hardcover sale, then went the way of most first novels— to the remainder table. But in reality, the publication of a book can hardly affect your life as profoundly as the writing of it. This went double for *Danny Slocum*, and over the years I've almost perversely felt more glad than sad that Danny and my connection with him seemed all but forgotten. The most enduring consequences of having written the book were letters— touching and funny, embarrassing and moving— I received from men who saw themselves in Danny.

Now *Danny Slocum* is getting a second chance and my feelings are mainly paternal. For in these five short years a pronounced generation gap has developed; unlike his titular father, certainly, Danny will never grow older, and the world he lives in seems dead as a dodo to me.

In Danny's inconclusive world, it's still three o'clock in the morning and the d.j. hasn't yet played his last "Last Dance." In that ghostly disco, it seems to me, hearts still throb with the kind of elation, expectation and even innocence most gay men of my generation will never be able to feel again. Countless of those hearts have been stilled forever. Danny might be wrestling with some weighty ironies, but he will never have to face the conundrum of sex and death that confronts us at present.

And yet—I can only hope you'll agree—Danny was never really, I think, searching for sex in the first place. Maybe for wholeness. He was a survivor and I feel somehow he'd find a way.

George Whitmore
New York City
December 1984

Other Grey Fox Books of Particular Interest